Alexia Ellery Finsdale

SAN FRANCISCO, 1905

⸻ ∞∞∞ ⸻

by Kathleen Duey

Book 7

⸻ ∞∞∞ ⸻

Aladdin Paperbacks

For Richard
For Ever

25 Years of Magical Reading

ALADDIN PAPERBACKS
EST. 1972

First Aladdin Paperbacks edition October 1997
Copyright © 1997 by Kathleen Duey

Aladdin Paperbacks
An imprint of Simon & Schuster
Children's Publishing Division
1230 Avenue of the Americas
New York, NY 10020

The text of this book was set in Fairfield Medium

Printed and bound in the United States of America
10 9 8 7 6 5 4 3 2 1

Library of Congress Cataloging-in-Publication Data
Duey, Kathleen.
Alexia Ellery Finsdale, San Francisco, 1905 / Kathleen Duey. —
1st Aladdin paperbacks ed.
p. cm. — (American diaries ; #7)
Summary: In San Francisco near the beginning of the twentieth century, Alexia faces a moral dilemma when her con man father tries to cheat the widow who has been like a mother to Alexia.
ISBN 0-689-81620-0 (pb)
[1. Fathers and daughters—Fiction. 2. Sewing—Fiction. 3. Swindlers and swindling—Fiction. 4. San Francisco (Calif.)—Fiction.] I. Title. II. Series.
PZ7.D8694Al 1997
[Fic]—dc21 97-24652
CIP AC

Still at Mrs. Tanner's Lodging House! A whole year since I began this diary!!

This is a wonderful morning. The fog is gone and the sun is bright. Mrs. Tanner doesn't want me downstairs in the shop until nine so I can steal a few minutes to write.

I am hoping to finish sewing my waist this week. It is more than I ever thought I could do—it is just lovely, two dozen pin tucks and the lace yoke—the sleeves fit perfectly first try, too. I am better and better with the machine, learning to treadle smoothly. My handwork is still uneven sometimes, but improving. Mrs. Tanner is the best landlady anyone ever had. She is wonderful to me. Her hands are worse late—her arthritis hurts her terribly—so I try to do everything I can to ease her work.

I haven't told Papa about the waist and skirt I am making. I suppose I had better tell soon, or someone else will. They have all seen me working on it in the shop. Cecil says he thinks it's the most beautiful bodice he has ever seen. Then, of course, *he blushes. If I could have an older brother, I would want him to be like Cecil.*

Misses Pleasant and Harvest went on and on about my sewing yesterday. They are so odd— here they are in their late forties, with graying hair—and still like two little girl twins who bicker and finish each other's sentences. Today they dressed alike as they usually do, laced up tight in their old hourglass, last-century corsets.

It has been a usual kind of morning. Mr. Chair and Cecil ate their oat porridge quickly and went to their work—as did Papa. Mr. Chair was off to Petaluma and points north to sell his line of boots and work shoes, Cecil still drives a wagon for Mr. Simmon's Freight Company.

Papa and Mrs. Tanner had another discussion at supper last night. He disapproves of her woman suffrage opinions and says she is in danger of losing her lady's delicacy the way she argues politics with Mr. Chair and him. I think she is always ladylike and kindhearted even when she discusses politics. That last bit is more than I can say for either Papa or Mr. Chair.

Women voting! It is hard to imagine. Papa says that the Southern Pacific Railroad runs California anyway, not the voters. Mrs. Tanner argues this.

She tried to play piano last week but her poor aching hands were too stiff and would not let her. She says she could try to teach me. Her hands are painful most of the time, I think. She does not complain and is impatient if I speak of it. She is very proud and wants no sympathy.

The sunlight is simply pouring in through the windows. It is hard to believe we have lived here a whole year. The only place we've ever stayed longer was at Mrs. Blackburn's in St. Louis, back when Mother was still alive. Someday I shall have to sit and write a list of every city I have seen. It will sound like the diary of a gypsy girl.

I realized recently that I love Mrs. Tanner as if she were an aunt, or part of a family I can only imagine. I barely recall Mother's sisters. Papa has never cared for Mother's family, and he says the Ellerys don't like him any better than he likes them. Since Father has no folks of his own, I will never know aunts or cousins—or even sisters and brothers, most likely. Papa is so handsome that women are attracted to him—but too many of the wrong kind. He says he isn't looking for another wife, anyway. But maybe even that can change now. Oh, it would be too wonderful if he would—so we could have a real family.

Yesterday a freight wagon brought cloth Mrs. Tanner had ordered through her fabric agent in New York City. Unpacking it was more fun than Christmas. There was cloud-soft Chinese silk of the most lovely blue and a heavy bolt of sea green moiré silk, also Chinese. Then there was milk-white linen from Ireland, and a crepeline of plum-colored silk that positively floats on the air.

Mrs. Tanner has made fancy gowns and stage costumes for every famous woman in the world, I think. Louisa Tetrazzini has worn her dresses on stage. So has Isadora Duncan. If Father knew that, he would probably forbid me to spend so much time with Mrs. Tanner! But Mrs. Tanner says that Miss Duncan is a whole new spirit of dance—that people just don't yet understand her artfulness.

I love it when Mrs. Tanner talks. Sometimes, listening, I feel as though I am going to be lifted off my feet and flown around the room. Yesterday I learned how to draft a gored skirt pattern. That is to say—I began to learn. It is so very hard. My waist has a boned collar. There is a lining, then an interlining, then, once it is basted down on the neckline, you have to work the cloth inside outward before you slide the bones in place. It is most tedious and troublesome, but Mrs. Tanner says that once I am good at it, it will seem easy as pie.

Oh, my. I hear Papa coming. His whistling gives him away. Why would he be here now, in the middle of the morning? Oh, how I hope nothing has gone wrong.

CHAPTER ONE

Alexia lifted her diary, swinging it briskly to dry the ink. The red silk cover was still perfect; not a single page was smudged. It held all her dreams and wishes and she took very good care of it.

Alexia could hear her father's whistling getting louder as he clumped up the stairs. She shook her head. Had something gone wrong at the printer's? She swung the diary back and forth a few more times, then looked. The ink had dulled—it was dry.

She opened her mother's trunk. Sliding the diary into its place between the folded tablecloths and the embroidered pillowcases, Alexia whirled around. Moving like a hummingbird darting along a honeysuckle hedge, she smoothed the bedspread, pushed her father's laundry bag under his bed, and squared up the stack of newspapers that always built up beside his nightstand. In twenty seconds the room looked fine, but she got out her dust rag.

By the time her father opened the door, Alexia was dusting. He came in grinning, leaving the door standing wide as he stepped into the room. His grin faded the instant he saw her.

"Alexia?" He looked startled. "I thought you would be downstairs by this time—with a hundred steel pins poking out of your mouth." He arched his brows and lifted both hands, making a theatrical expression of surprise.

Then, still acting like a man in a play, he sat on the edge of the bed and made a treadle motion with his feet, pretending to sew. He hummed a little to himself—something that Mrs. Tanner often did when she was sewing something difficult. The look of fierce concentration on his face was comical as he acted the part of a seamstress trying to make everything come out straight. He picked up a sheet of newspaper—part of yesterday's *Chronicle*, and waved it about, miming Mrs. Tanner when she shook the wrinkles out of her rice-paper pattern pieces.

Alexia couldn't help but laugh. He stood and

took a mock bow, bending to kiss the top of her head. Alexia loved it when he was funny like this. He looked very handsome in his dark suit and tan waistcoat. He had gotten his wavy brown hair barbered a few days before and had used bay rum this morning. He smelled sweet and spicy and his even, white teeth winked beneath his thick brown mustache.

"What?" he asked, arching his brows even higher. "What are you looking at? Is my collar buttoned unevenly or something?"

Alexia laughed again at the face he made, his eyes widening as though an unbuttoned collar was a horror he could not face. "No, Papa, I was just thinking that you're handsome."

"Am I?" He turned sideways, preening like a vain girl. He grinned at her rakishly and Alexia felt a sudden wariness in her heart. Why was he being so silly? Sometimes he was just in a silly mood but . . . . She narrowed her eyes. Had he been drinking?

He was still grinning. "Is that sour-faced old suffragist filling your head with her foolishness while you work down there? Because if she is—"

"Papa, don't," Alexia interrupted, speaking very softly so he wouldn't get angry at her disrespect. "Please. Mrs. Tanner is very good to me. She just wants me to be able to make my way in the world if

I must."

Her father shook his head. "You just marry well and we won't have any such need, will we?" He swayed, just a little, on his feet. Alexia crossed her fingers behind her back and said a silent prayer. He hadn't been going to saloons much since he had gotten the print shop position. A whole year. It seemed like an eternity ago that she had last seen him truly intoxicated. And he hadn't been in trouble with the police for that long—he hadn't even come up with one of his schemes—so far as she knew, anyway.

Alexia studied her father's face. He cupped her chin in his hand. "You are a lovely girl. You will soon be a beautiful young woman. The only difficulty you will have will be choosing from the throngs of young men who come to court you."

Alexia stepped back. "Papa, please. It is good that I am learning something more than how to mop up a floor, isn't it?"

"Of course," he agreed instantly. "I just don't want you to start spouting all that progressive nonsense—about women getting the vote and all the rest."

"Papa, I just—"

"I forgot my wallet." Her father interrupted, as though he was just remembering. He pulled his big gold watch from his waistcoat pocket and looked at it. "And if I don't hurry, I'll be late."

Alexia felt a familiar tightness in her stomach. "Late? For what?"

She waited as her father looked at his watch a second time, then put it back in his waistcoat before looking at her. When he did, his eyes were steady, intent. "I will be late getting back to the print shop, of course. I told Mr. Higgins I would return promptly."

Alexia stood back as he opened his wardrobe and began going through the inner drawer, his back to her. A few seconds later he straightened up, but it was a long moment before he turned around to face her—and when he did, his hands were empty.

"Perhaps I took it after all and just put it in my desk at the shop."

Alexia averted her eyes and nodded. "Perhaps."

Her father came across the room and embraced her quickly, hugging her against his chest for a second, then releasing her. He turned to go back to the door.

"I will see you at noon for dinner, Alexia," he said, winking. "I am arranging a wonderful surprise. So don't let anything upset you before then, Fairy Princess. And don't swallow any of those pins."

She met his eyes. He hadn't used her old nick-name in so long that it made her feel like a little girl just to hear it. Fairy Princess. It had been her mother's name for her from the time she was born. Her real name had come from a story her mother had read.

Alexia sighed, looking at her father. His smile was irresistible and she smiled back. He touched his forehead in a mock salute, then went out. Halfway down the stairs, he started whistling again.

Alexia stood very still until she heard the front door open and close. Then she sat down on the edge of the bed. The mattress springs squeaked beneath her weight.

"It doesn't mean anything," she said aloud. "He said he had forgotten his wallet, but he had just made a mistake, that's all."

Alexia stood up quickly, turning in a slow circle, looking at everything in their room. Her mother's trunk was easily the handsomest object in it. The rest of the cheap furniture had been gotten at freighters' damaged goods auctions down on Market Street.

Every possession that mattered to Alexia was in the trunk. The linens had been her mother's and her grandmother's. Most of them bore precise, pretty embroidery. The red silk diary was a gift from her father, bought one giddy day last summer—the day they had found Mrs. Tanner's boardinghouse.

They had been forced to leave their last lodging house and Alexia's father had been furious with Mr. Wilkins at first. He had ranted and raved as they walked, and finally Alexia had stopped listening. Then, as always, he had begun to whistle and smile as they searched for another place to live. Alexia didn't ask what had gone wrong. At least the police didn't seem to be involved.

Once they found Mrs. Tanner's, and she agreed to let them move in without advance rent, Alexia's father had been jubilant and had insisted they celebrate. They had ridden cable cars all over, then somehow they had ended up in a dim, scented shop in Chinatown.

The diary still smelled faintly of Chinese incense. The old man who had sold it to them told them it contained great luck—it would bring good fortune to Alexia for as long as she kept it. So far it had, she realized. At least, until today it had.

"Papa won't do anything that will make us have to move again," Alexia whispered to herself. "He said he would keep his job this time—that he wouldn't try to make easy money or gamble. He promised." She felt the sting of tears in her eyes. She jumped to her feet and went to the window.

On the porch below, Mrs. Tanner's big black-and-white tomcat, Perseus, was curled up in a chair.

Across the street her father was walking briskly past the untrimmed lilac hedge that bordered the lot opposite Mrs. Tanner's. Alexia could tell by the jaunty tilt to his head that he was still whistling. Alexia held her breath, watching as he got closer to the eucalyptus tree that overhung the cobblestone street at the corner.

If he were really going straight back to work, he would turn left at the corner, and head toward Eighth Street to catch the cable car to the print shop.

As he got close to the intersection, Alexia crossed her fingers, pressing her face against the cool glass. She watched as her father hesitated at the curb. Then he turned right.

CHAPTER TWO

"Alexia?"

Startled, Alexia stumbled back from the window. Mrs. Tanner's voice had come from the hallway. "Coming," Alexia called out. Fumbling with the slick glass knob, wiping her eyes, Alexia managed a smile as she opened the door.

Mrs. Tanner was rubbing one hand with the other. Her knuckles always looked swollen because of her arthritis. She was wearing a heavily plaited walking toilette that Alexia had never seen before. It was a somber dark green, the wool challis draped perfectly. Mrs. Tanner made all of her own clothes, of course.

"I wasn't expecting you," Alexia said politely. "Did you change your mind about starting early today?"

"Not exactly," Mrs. Tanner said, looking past her into the room. "I saw your father downstairs and asked him if you could accompany me on an errand. He gave his permission."

Alexia felt her stomach tighten. Had Mrs. Tanner noticed that Papa had been drinking? "He forgot his wallet," she said quickly. "He had to hurry back."

Mrs. Tanner reached out and touched her cheek. "Well, then. I wondered why he was home. That explains it."

Alexia nodded, searching Mrs. Tanner's face. Something was wrong, she was sure of it. But what? Was her father up to something?

"Would you like to come with me?" Mrs. Tanner asked. She paused dramatically. "When we get back you are going to cut the muslin for Mrs. Todd's gown—the one she will wear to Mrs. Hearst's ball. It is to be a cotillion with dancing and the most clever favors."

Alexia caught her breath. Mrs. Tanner often made a whole toilette from muslins—using lightweight nainsook from India where silk would later be used—to work out details before she cut into the fine fabric she would use for the finished dress.

Alexia felt a little light-headed and tried not to giggle. It was amazing. *She* was going to help make a gown for a ball at the Hearst mansion? "Mrs. Hearst is famous," Alexia said.

"Mrs. Hearst is an angel," Mrs. Tanner said. "A feisty angel with potfuls of money and energy for good causes. With women of her social position behind woman suffrage, it will not be denied forever."

Alexia ducked her head, hoping that Mrs. Tanner would not get started talking about women voting. Or temperance. Or women's rights before the law. It was all interesting, exciting talk—but disturbing, too. Sometimes it seemed to Alexia that the world was changing too fast. She was sick of changes. She just wanted to stay at Mrs. Tanner's and learn how to be a seamstress. All she wanted was for everything to stay the same forever—and she knew it wouldn't.

"Are you ready?" Mrs. Tanner asked. Alexia looked up, distracted from her unhappy thoughts. "Alexia? Is something wrong? Has your father told you about the difficulty? It will be worked out, I assure you."

Mrs. Tanner's manner was kind and patient

as always. But her words tightened the knot in Alexia's stomach.

"What difficulty?"

Mrs. Tanner reacted instantly. "Oh, dear. He didn't tell you, did he? And now I have. I apologize, Alexia. I have made an awful mistake."

She looked so upset that Alexia shook her head. "It's fine. I just . . . what's wrong?"

Mrs. Tanner was rubbing her hands together. "Nothing that your father won't take care of as quickly as he can, I am sure." She touched Alexia's cheek. "I really have spoken unwisely."

"Is he behind in our rent?" Alexia pleaded. "Is he?" She could feel her own heartbeat. He had promised this would never happen again—that he would keep his position this time. Alexia blinked and an image of her father whistling down the street rose in her mind. *Right*. He had turned right, toward the saloons and restaurants that lined Howard Street.

"I am going to suggest to him that he let me apply your wages against the rent—rather than just giving him the money. Perhaps that will help him—" Mrs. Tanner broke off, obviously uncomfortable and angry with herself.

"I will be down in just a moment," Alexia said as evenly as she could.

Mrs. Tanner nodded as politely as Alexia had spoken, but her eyes were full of distress. Alexia stepped back from the door, waiting until Mrs. Tanner had turned to go down the hallway before she closed it. Then she stood leaning against the door, staring at nothing.

He had done it again. He had ruined everything. How *could* he? Hands shaking, Alexia paced the length of the room, then walked back to stand before the window. She stared out at the sunny morning, then glanced at her mother's trunk, remembering the diary entry she had written just a few minutes before.

Alexia lowered her head. Well, now it wasn't such a wonderful morning, was it? Her father was doing what he had always done. He was probably spending the money they both earned to drink too much—and probably to gamble. Maybe he had lost it all in some risky scheme. And now he would look for ways to make it back.

"The first time he comes back to the house smelling strongly enough of whiskey, Mrs. Tanner will be asking us to leave," Alexia whispered aloud. "Or maybe she will throw us out for back rent if he has let it get bad enough already." She clenched her fists and dug her fingernails into her palms until tears stopped stinging her eyes. What had he said? Not to let anything upset her? Maybe he had a solution. Maybe this time he would figure something out.

"I have to go downstairs now," Alexia told herself. "I have to work hard and be helpful and clever and maybe Mrs. Tanner will let us stay." Alexia closed her eyes and repeated the words three or four times with her fingers crossed behind her back. She knew it didn't work. It had never worked, but she still did it, just as she had when she was little.

"Excuse me? Alexia, dear?"

Alexia whirled to face the closed door. "Yes, Mrs. Tanner?"

"You'll need your cloak. It's brisk and damp this morning."

"Thank you," Alexia called.

After a moment Alexia opened the door a crack. Mrs. Tanner was gone. She opened the door a little wider, peeking out before she stepped into the reception room that all the tenants shared. She crossed the deep red carpet quickly, glancing across at the twins' door, hoping that they wouldn't choose this particular moment to come out. Mr. Chair and Cecil were gone, of course—they had used the washroom and the water closet early, long before sunrise. Their doors were side by side on the back wall of the reception room.

The hallway that led to the washroom was short. The door stood ajar, the house signal that it was empty. The water closet was across the hall. Its door was always closed and Alexia hated knocking. Usually she just kept an eye out long enough to be nearly certain no one was inside before she even approached the door.

Alexia slipped inside the washroom and turned up the gas lamp on the wall. The gas hissed a little, then the flame popped and stretched upward. The little mirror above the basin was clouded with age and mildew, but Alexia could still see that her face looked pink.

The shiny nickel-plated spigot was hard to turn and Alexia leaned forward to get a better grip. Bringing her face that close to the mirror, she saw that her eyes were red from rubbing.

"Papa will get another position if something has happened at the print shop," she told her image, then filled her cupped hands with the cold water and bent down to splash her face. She used the soap on her hands and throat, then rinsed, careful not to spatter her bodice. It was getting too tight, she knew. She needed another cotton everyday frock soon. That's what she should be making, not the beautiful silk waist and skirt that she would never be able to wear to school.

The cotton towels were hanging on wall pegs. Alexia used her own to dry herself. Then she leaned close to the mirror again. "Better," she told herself. It was almost impossible now to tell that she had been on the verge of tears. Alexia absolutely didn't want Mrs. Tanner to see that she had been that upset. Perhaps it was only this month's rent of eight dollars. They could catch that up if they were careful for a few months. Maybe instead of keeping the dress she was making for herself, she could sell it through Mrs. Tanner's shop. Mrs. Tanner had said it was almost professional quality, hadn't she? It would be worth two dollars, perhaps. Or even three.

Alexia looked at herself in the mirror again, practicing a smile.

"Is someone in there?"

Alexia's smile stiffened. It was one of the twins—Alexia couldn't tell which. She wiped at her eyes one last time to make sure all the traces of tears were gone, then turned to the door. Even once she had opened it and was looking into the vague blue eyes, she still wasn't sure which twin she was talking to.

"I wasn't sure if someone was in there or if Mr. Chair had simply closed the door when he left again. He is just so terrible about the door. I can't imagine why."

Alexia inclined her head—acknowledging without agreeing. She liked Mr. Chair, but she knew that the twins didn't—especially Harvest. He was a shoe salesman, gone most of the time, riding his route all the way up into Petaluma and beyond. Harvest thought he was common, because sometimes he used words like "ain't" and "swell." Pleasant didn't like him because he insisted on telling them, once or twice a week, how remarkable their resemblance was. As Pleasant said, that was hardly headline news at this point in their lives.

"Have I rushed you, Alexia?"

"I am quite finished . . ." Alexia hesitated, wondering if she should risk a guess, then decided not to. Miss Pleasant never minded if she was mistaken, but Miss Harvest was always offended.

"I'm Pleasant." The vague blue eyes twinkled a little and the older woman ran a hand over her smooth chignon. "My mother used to say that I was, anyway. Harvest was a more difficult child."

Alexia smiled at the joke. She had heard it several times now. "I am sorry to have kept you waiting, Miss Pleasant."

"Not at all, Alexia," Miss Pleasant assured her. "Are you off with Mrs. Tanner?"

Alexia smiled. The twins always seemed to know about everything that was going on in the boardinghouse.

"I saw your father come home," Miss Pleasant said as Alexia stepped out of the washroom. Alexia stopped, her heart speeding up a little. She did not want to have to fib and hoped Miss Pleasant wouldn't ask her questions.

"He is such a handsome man," Miss Pleasant said. There was a wistful tone in her voice and Alexia smiled. "He cuts quite a figure," Miss Pleasant added.

Alexia nodded, then excused herself. She threw one glance back over her shoulder and Miss Pleasant waved, a quick flutter of her long, graceful fingers.

Alexia walked down the hall, then across the reception room, with its heavy Morris chairs lined up against the wall.

Alexia smiled as Perseus came trotting across the carpet to rub against her leg. She bent to scratch his silky chin. As he tilted his head and began to purr, she thrust her worry-thoughts aside. Everything was going to be all right. It just had to be.

CHAPTER THREE

Back in her room Alexia smoothed her bodice over her corset and wished for the hundredth time that she had a real one, not just the *healthy* one Mrs. Tanner had given her. There wasn't much boning in it at all—and only one layer of the coutil fabric. Certainly not enough to shape her figure into the beautiful S shape of a proper Grecian bend—even if it had been bent correctly, which it wasn't. Alexia's corset had a flat busk down the front, the metal thin and almost flexible.

Mrs. Tanner said the Grecian bend was unnatural and ugly, and that Madam Gauches-Sorret had done women a great service designing a health corset. But Alexia liked the way the fashionable women looked, with their hips tilted forward and their spines arched, all the while throwing their shoulders back and standing erect.

Walking past her mother's trunk, Alexia brushed her fingers across the wood bows in the lid. Her father always said that her mother had a tiny waist that, laced, had been small enough for him to put his hands around. Alexia sighed. Sometimes she still missed her mother so badly it was like a physical ache—an old bruise she kept injuring so it couldn't quite heal.

Alexia lifted her cloak from its hook beside the door and took down her hat from its shelf in her wardrobe. It was old, and it needed retrimming. She had found the spray of red silk flowers in Mrs. Tanner's rubbish bin nearly a year before. The ribbons were from Mrs. Tanner's garniture remnants. One of these days she would have to save up to buy some new ribbons or more flowers—or maybe a little bit of lace would work.

Alexia went out the door and stood in the reception room, composing herself. She noticed a white rectangle on the red carpet near the top of the stairs. Mrs. Tanner had left a note in front of her apartment door.

Alexia dear,
I have run down into the shop.
Meet me there, if you will, please.
Mrs. A. H. Tanner

Alexia liked Mrs. Tanner's big ornate hand-writing. Her father said it looked like a man's hand more than a woman's—because of the loops and flourishes and its boldness. Alexia folded the note and slipped it into her pocket.

She started down the stairs, wondering what her married name would be. Mrs. Tanner's husband, August Tanner, had died a long time ago. The *H* stood for Herbert—his middle name. Mrs. Tanner's name was Lydia. Alexia thought it was lovely—it sounded like water over stones, smooth and rippling.

Alexia wondered for a moment if her mother would have liked Mrs. Tanner. Maybe not. Papa always said her mother had been very conservative and old-fashioned.

Going across the yard, Alexia took a deep breath and looked up at the sky, then shrugged her cloak a little higher on her shoulders. It was soft, warm, made of thick boiled wool. Mrs. Tanner had helped her make it, using some light gray fabric she had left from a riding skirt she had made for a client. Alexia fingered the guipure lace that edged the neckline. This cloak was finer than anything she had ever expected to own—and she had made it herself. She had even drafted the pattern. It was a simple one, of course, only five pieces.

"You're daydreaming, aren't you?" Mrs. Tanner teased from the shop door. Alexia ducked her head, blushing as Mrs. Tanner laughed. "Oh, I am only fooling, Alexia. I'm in no hurry today. In fact, I would rather do almost anything than face that bolt of plum silk."

"For Miss Helm's walking dress?"

Mrs. Tanner smiled. "Yes. And since it has finally arrived from New York, I have no further excuse for putting off cutting it. The muslin sewed up perfectly, right down to those hellish, outdated corkscrew sleeves she insists upon. I only had to adjust the scye and the back depth of the basque— and each of those less than a quarter inch." Mrs. Tanner began rubbing her hands together. It was an absentminded gesture, an automatic one. "I must be getting lazy. I almost dread beginning a long job like this one."

Alexia forced herself not to stare at Mrs. Tanner's hands. She knew it wasn't the intricate cutting or sewing that Mrs. Tanner really dreaded. It was the pain in her poor knuckles and wrists while she worked. It certainly wasn't any form of laziness, Alexia knew. Mrs. Tanner was the very soul of energy and industry.

"So. I will need silk thread," Mrs. Tanner said. "And I think we'll go to The White House this time and see what they have. I just want to cut a piece of the fabric so that we can make sure of a match." Mrs. Tanner ducked back inside the shop.

Alexia opened the door a little wider and stood just inside it, waiting. The shop always smelled faintly of Mrs. Tanner's lavender-scented soap. Alexia looked at the five dressmakers' mannequins that stood side by side along the back wall. Two were slim, two stout—one of each was long waisted and the other was short waisted. They were old, all but one imported from Europe.

Mrs. Tanner used the dress forms for her clients—but only as a rough reference as work progressed. Each garment she made was measured against the woman herself. Sometimes the measuring tapes and sliding arm measuring square were used several times between the first fitting and the last. Mrs. Tanner was a perfectionist. That was why so many discriminating women depended upon her.

"Once we have finished at The White House, we can walk up to Robinson's Pet Shop on Bush and Kearny if you like," Mrs. Tanner said as she fiddled with the pins that held the plum silk fabric tightly on its bolt.

"I love to look at the little monkeys," Alexia said eagerly.

Mrs. Tanner nodded, rubbing the cloth between two fingers. "As do I. But as precious as they are with their little hands and human faces, I someday want to own a green parrot—and teach it to talk."

Alexia made a sound of agreement, but her eyes were drifting back to the mannequins. She stared at the last mannequin in the line. It was slender—a girl's form. On it, nearly finished, was the waist Mrs. Tanner was helping her sew.

The fabric glowed like candlelight—not quite amber, not quite rose. The lace was pinned in place on the boned collar, a dove gray that contrasted just enough with the silk to make each detail stand out.

Mrs. Tanner had helped her draft the pattern—just from looking at the drawing in the August issue of the *Delineator*. It was a wonderful toilette, with a gored skirt and the new slimmer sleeves.

Alexia sighed. It was going to be beautiful—if she could somehow manage the fifteen intricate gores in the skirt and the plaits at the hemline. It would be much too fine for her to ever wear.

"Bring a sliver of your silk, too," Mrs. Tanner said, pointing toward the scrap box. Alexia fished out a small swatch of the silk and put it in her pocket.

"Why?"

Mrs. Tanner smiled. "You never know what you'll see."

Alexia watched Mrs. Tanner lay the plum silk out across the cutting table. Her shears were lined up neatly on the edge of an ornate old sideboard against the wall that she used as a tool table. She selected the long-bladed steel pair and slid them beneath the fabric, cutting a sliver so slender that it fluttered to the floor.

"This is one of the nicest crepelines I have ever seen," Mrs. Tanner said as Alexia bent to pick up the scrap of fabric. "I do believe that Mr. Gotts carries the nicest silks now. Mr. Bettcher used to have my favorite line of fabrics, but he seems to have lost his reliable Chinese contact. But Gotts is so slow."

"You waited nearly three months for this order," Alexia said, remembering how upset the client had been when her dress had been delayed. She picked up the bolt and held the plum-colored cloth up to the light that came in the front windows. It was gossamer, sheer as mist.

"The silver lamé will gleam through this like coins through wine," Mrs. Tanner said. "And it will positively float as she moves. I want to look at The White House for a velvet for the piping and trim. I was going to use black, just for a touch of midnight here and there. But now I think a deeper plum would work better. If I can find one light enough I may piece in a panel or two in the skirt." She sighed, touching her hair, patting the stray strands back into her chignon. Then she rubbed her hands together again. "We need to finish your waist this week. I think we can."

Alexia crossed the shop to look at her bodice. The major construction sewing had been done. "I can cut the sleeves tomorrow once I have finished with other work," Alexia said impulsively. Then she hesitated. Mrs. Tanner had every right to expect her to work extra hours if her father was behind with rent. But Mrs. Tanner was nodding.

"I am looking forward to it. And once the bodice is finished, we can begin on the skirt. A gored skirt is a landmark for every young seamstress."

"Thank you, Mrs. Tanner," Alexia said. She searched for a way to tell Mrs. Tanner how much her kindness meant.

"Well," Mrs. Tanner said briskly into the silence. "Shall we go? We could catch a cable car up on Market, but Union Square isn't all that far and I think the walk would do us both good."

Alexia smiled. Mrs. Tanner always thought the walk to the department stores would do them both good. The truth was she hated to spend even a few cents on fare. After all, she was a woman alone, a widow, making her own way. She had no money to spare.

"You don't mind walking, do you?" Mrs. Tanner asked as she stood in front of the shop mirrors, repinning her hat. It was a wide-brimmed affair today, trimmed with grosgrain ribbon and a spray of silk roses.

Alexia shook her head. She really didn't mind. It was probably not much more than a mile and a half and she was used to walking. She never had enough money for a cable car ticket anyway. Sometimes her father gave her a nickel back from her week's wages, but he often forgot.

"All right, then." Mrs. Tanner picked up her handbag and took one last look in the mirror. She was not vain, Alexia knew. She hated her tightest corsets and would happily have worn only the barest restraints—just enough for decency. But she dressed up when she went to shop. She was her own best advertisement.

Mrs. Tanner's clothing was impeccable, so unusually well styled that women often turned on the streets to watch her pass. A few even asked where she had her dresses made. Then she could, with all due modesty, explain that she was a modiste and had made what she was wearing. She carried calling cards with her name and the shop address.

Mrs. Tanner led the way out and across the narrow strip of the front yard, shooing Perseus back to the porch when he tried to follow them. She turned left, and Alexia followed. Their heels clicked on the cobblestones as they walked northeast on Langton.

Mrs. Tanner's posture was perfectly erect, as always, her steps firm and purposeful. Without being obvious about it, Alexia dropped back a half step and tried to mimic her high-headed graceful walk—but with a little more of the fashionable S curve in her own posture. When she grew up, she wanted to carry herself well, just as Mrs. Tanner did.

"That cloak is perfect with your dark hair," Mrs. Tanner said, pausing beneath the huge eucalyptus tree on the corner of Howard Street. Alexia felt herself blushing as Mrs. Tanner started off again, turning right, stepping up onto the concrete sidewalk.

"Oh, how the young men are going to gather on my porch in a few years if you and your father are still staying at my house," Mrs. Tanner teased. Her eyes were twinkling.

Alexia looked aside. *If they were still staying at her house.* Maybe Mrs. Tanner was breaking the news to her that they might have to move. It would be like her to try to say it in a kind way.

"Whatever is wrong with you today?" Mrs. Tanner asked. "You are quiet as a mouse. Is it what I said about the rent? I apologize again. I should never have said anything to you."

Alexia shook her head, unable to answer. She wanted to ask how far in arrears her father had fallen. She wanted to ask how much money it would take to set everything straight again. But she was afraid to.

Alexia made a show of straightening her cloak. What if it was so much that there was no hope of ever catching up? Alexia turned to hide the despair she knew showed on her face. It was always like this with her father. Either they fell behind on rent, or he cheated someone with a fast deal of some kind.

Alexia walked fast—she had to keep up with Mrs. Tanner's energetic stride. They passed through a group of shouting boys rolling hoops at a breakneck pace along the sidewalk. The boys scattered to let Alexia and Mrs. Tanner pass, leaping up into yards on one side and down into the street on the other. Then they closed into a pack again, laughing. Alexia watched them race away, three of them using their T-shaped sticks to lift the hoops, bouncing them off a long sign advertising Jessee Moore Whiskey.

"Alexia?"

Alexia looked sidelong at Mrs. Tanner.

"I wish I could take back my words," Mrs. Tanner said softly, slowing her step a little so that they walked side by side. "I mentioned the rent because I thought you knew. I did not intend to upset you like this."

Alexia stared straight ahead, unable to think of a single sensible word in answer. She had never told Mrs. Tanner about her father—about the many places they had lived and all the midnight departures when things got rough. And she didn't want to tell her now. It would only convince her that there was little chance of the back rent ever getting paid.

Mrs. Tanner hesitated on the corner of Seventh Street, looking up the block toward the beautiful new post office. She smiled. "I am expecting an important package. I wonder if we should go check on it now."

"Then we would have to carry it or take it back to the shop," Alexia said, glad of the distraction from their uneasy conversation.

"Of course, you're right," Mrs. Tanner said. She nodded and turned to lead the way straight up

Howard Street again. "It's a box of ribbons from Chicago," she explained as they went on. "The woman is so unreliable. She wrote to tell me she would finally be sending them this week. I hope she is being truthful with me."

Mrs. Tanner glanced at Alexia. Alexia met her eyes and saw only the usual friendly regard in them. Maybe Mrs. Tanner wouldn't make them move. Maybe there was some way she could work more hours, and some way to keep the extra money out of her father's hands. That was going to be the hardest part. After all, every penny of her wages belonged to him. If he saw fit to drink them away, invest them in a bank, or throw them at the moon, it was his right.

CHAPTER FOUR

Alexia kept looking around, scanning the faces of people who stood outside the boardinghouses and saloons. Was her father somewhere close? If she saw him standing by a saloon, what would she do? Pretend she hadn't seen him?

Alexia stepped off the curb and into the street to avoid two dogs that circled each other, growling. Mrs. Tanner was a half step ahead. She smiled and glanced back at Alexia. "Something must be done about the dogs in this neighborhood. Every transient who stays a few months seems to want a dog—then leaves it for the rest of us."

"Dog fight!" someone shouted.

Alexia heard Mrs. Tanner make a sound of disapproval. Men were streaming out of a small saloon that occupied the lowest floor of the Ohio House. Some came out of the Lormor as well. One man in a flannel shirt and bright red braces was fishing bills from his trouser pocket. They were going to bet on the fight, Alexia realized.

As the dogs snapped and snarled, men began leaving the Kingsbury and Mr. Peacock's restaurant on the ground floor of the Girard House farther up the street. Most went on their way after a few seconds, but some joined the crowd forming around the dogs. Many wore workman's trousers and rough shirts, but others had nice dark suits with watch chains looped across their waistcoats. There were one or two women—loose, frowsy-looking women who hung around saloons asking for drinks. Since it was illegal to serve them inside, they had to talk a man into buying whiskey for them—or go to a saloon fancy enough to have a women's section.

"Keep your eyes ahead, Alexia," Mrs. Tanner cautioned. "If people must do despicable things, at least we should not give them the satisfaction of watching them."

Alexia looked back once more at the dogs

and the crowd gathering around them, then glanced at Mrs. Tanner's face. She was flushed now, angry. Alexia knew that any cruelty to animals upset her. So did gambling and drinking. But she wasn't sour-faced, Alexia knew, no matter what her father said. Mrs. Tanner loved a good joke. And she loved dancing and music and opera and plays. It was a mean trick of fate that the building her father had left her was here, south of Mission, in a district that made her face—daily—everything she loathed.

"They were about to fight anyway," Alexia said, hoping to ease the strain on Mrs. Tanner's face. "They will probably just nip and snarl a while, then each will go its way."

"But the crowd will make it worse. Their circle will keep one from running away when it wants to. If they have to, they'll shove the dogs at each other. I hate liquor and the excesses it fosters."

Alexia nodded vaguely, thinking about her father. Drinking always seemed to get him into trouble of one kind or another.

Mrs. Tanner was frowning. "It is the beer and whiskey companies financing the resistance to woman suffrage, Alexia. They are scared to death that if we get the vote we will make their products illegal. And we just might." She tossed her head, indicating the men behind them. "There are few women who have not been harmed by liquor. Nearly everyone has a brother or an uncle or a cousin who would be a better man without drink."

Alexia nodded again, wondering if Mrs. Tanner had any idea that her father drank. Probably not, she decided. He had only rarely indulged since they had lived at Mrs. Tanner's. Alexia lifted her skirt a fraction of an inch and pretended to concentrate on making sure the cloth stayed clear of the sidewalk where a cracked water main was leaking into the gutter.

"Hey there, Mrs. Tanner! Hello, Alexia!"

The voice was loud and jovial. Alexia glanced up to see Jack, the ice wagon driver who delivered ice to the boardinghouse. She waved.

Jack's white mules were plodding along as they always did, their neat little hooves as small as ponies'. Jack kept them clean and groomed—and the harness shone. His cousin owned several grocery stores and the icehouse. Jack's real name was Giovani, but he said that he had a new country, so why not a new name, too? He always gave Alexia splinters of ice to suck on when the weather was hot. As usual, he was beaming, his teeth crooked but very white.

"Now there is an example of manhood and humankind one can admire," Mrs. Tanner said, smiling back.

Jack doffed his cap and grinned, pulling the wagon close to the curb to stop. "My wife says to thank you with all of her heart for the gift."

"I sent along some good wool I had no immediate use for," Mrs. Tanner explained quickly to Alexia. "The client changed her mind and wanted linen." She turned to Jack. "You tell her that I hope she wears it in good health."

"I will, ma'am." Jack lifted his cap a second time and glanced at Alexia, including her in his sunny grin and his farewell. He clucked to the mules and they leaned into the harness, pulling the neatly painted wagon on down the street.

"I only wish that the whole world could be peopled by families like that one. His wife works harder than anyone I know. His children are clean and polite. I wish I had apartments large enough for big families. Just a little bigger, I mean. Nothing so grand as the Bella Vista down on California Street."

Alexia turned around, pretending to look after Jack, but trying to see what had happened with the dogs. It was impossible. The circle of men was complete now. They stood shoulder to shoulder, laughing and shouting. Was her father there instead of at work? She sighed.

"What is it?" Mrs. Tanner asked.

Alexia turned. There was such a look of concern on Mrs. Tanner's face that she reached out to touch her hand. "Nothing. I'm just worried."

Mrs. Tanner looked into her eyes. "Your father told me last night that something is coming up for him. Some opportunity. He would say no more than that."

Alexia ducked her head. She could only guess whether there was a real opportunity or if he had just said it to stave off Mrs. Tanner's inquiry about her rent. "I don't know what he is planning to do," Alexia said quietly, then cleared her throat. "I imagine he will tell me about it at dinner today, or perhaps this evening."

Mrs. Tanner took Alexia's hand. "I am sure he will tell us both when there is something to tell." She touched Alexia's cheek. "And that's enough talk about it. It is making you positively gray around the edges. You will learn as you get older that worry rarely helps anything, including the worrier."

Alexia nodded. Mrs. Tanner gestured up the street. "Look. I think that's the new young woman who will be teaching at the Lincoln School this coming autumn—she came all the way from Illinois."

Alexia followed Mrs. Tanner's gesture. Ahead of them, a young woman in a dark dress swayed along, parasol carried daintily in one hand. Her corset was properly tight, her back arched, tilting her hips forward into a very respectable Grecian bend.

"She looks as if she is about to fall down," Mrs. Tanner said under her breath. "I will be ever so glad when the mode changes. This posture cannot be good for women. And those corsets. There have been deaths from corsets."

Alexia stared at Mrs. Tanner, astonished. "Deaths?"

Mrs. Tanner nodded. "Yes. Mysterious deaths of young women. And the autopsies showed that their livers were actually divided in half."

Alexia watched the woman a half block ahead of them as she turned to look across the street.

"See that?" Mrs. Tanner pressed. "Her waist is compressed to eighteen or nineteen inches—no more than that. Where do you think her organs go when they are shoved inward like that?"

Alexia swallowed, feeling a little ill. Her own corset suddenly felt too tight.

"Think about the Chinese with their small-footed women who can barely walk. Or the Arabs with their veiled women fainting in the summer heat. It is all nonsense, Alexia."

Alexia had once seen a Chinese woman with feet so tiny she could barely hobble. "Papa said they bind their feet in rags when they are infants to keep them from growing," she said aloud.

Mrs. Tanner nodded. "People say the binders double the foot back under itself when the bones are soft. And that the little girl babies live in pain. They are in pain all their lives."

Alexia felt a wave of nausea again, remembering the crippled, strained walk of the small-footed woman. She had used two carved walking sticks and had been leaning on a servant for support. "Why would anyone bind a girl's feet?"

"It's not much different from that," Mrs. Tanner responded, nodding discreetly toward the young teacher who was mincing her way across the street now, her step careful. "You could teach one day," Mrs. Tanner said suddenly.

Alexia nodded automatically, then shook her head. "My father says I must marry well, then I won't have to worry about anything."

"I married well," Mrs. Tanner said, a little sharply. "It doesn't always mean money or safety."

Alexia glanced away, feeling foolish.

"My dear husband died and left me penniless after the doctors took their share, and his brothers. If it hadn't been for that old lodging house—and my sewing machine—"

"You are a famous modiste," Alexia said, smiling.

Mrs. Tanner smiled back. "Famous is too strong a word. But I can and do earn my own way. I can't tell you what a comfort and a satisfaction that is."

Alexia was watching Mrs. Tanner's face. She looked almost radiant, like a woman talking about love. Alexia imagined being grown up—without a husband. She had never thought about it before. It felt odd to think about it. Certainly no woman would choose a life like that.

At the corner of Sixth Street, Mrs. Tanner crossed over, then turned left. She paused as they passed Nicholas Prost's bakery, inhaling deeply, her eyes shining like a child's. There was a wonderful air of fresh bread and the delicate scent of sugar and butter from the pastries.

Alexia's mouth watered and, for a moment, she thought that Mrs. Tanner was going to suggest that they go in, but then she walked on and Alexia followed. The smell of baking gave way to the scents of lemon oil and sawdust as they passed a furniture warehouse.

"I read in the *Chronicle* that Louisa Tetrazzini is going to sing in San Francisco again soon," Mrs. Tanner said as they crossed Natoma Street. "If she can clear up the legal mess about her contract. If she does sing, we shall go. She has a voice like angels must have."

A few blocks up, the banging sputter of an automobile made Alexia look up. Some wealthy family was out for a ride. She listened, hoping that the sound would come closer, but it didn't. It faded. She was disappointed. Autos were so strange looking with their spindly little tires and their clumsy steering wheels.

"I shall never get used to looking at them," Mrs. Tanner said, as though reading Alexia's thought. "Just going along like that with nothing pulling them."

Alexia lifted her skirts to clear a puddle that looked like spilled milk. "Papa says they are a fashion that will not last long."

"Not if they can't make them cheaper," Mrs. Tanner agreed, raising her own hem to step over the spill. "But think of the freedom of it. No horses to feed, no liveryman to hire, no stable to build. I think most people would want to own one, if they could manage the price."

Alexia laughed. "They are no more than a rich man's toy, Papa says."

Mrs. Tanner stepped to one side, catching at Alexia's sleeve to pull her close as a file of roller-skating boys sped past. One of them touched his cap and nodded to Alexia. She blushed and looked down.

"Well, we shall see who's right as time goes on, won't we? I really think there will be more of those noisy machines than horses in twenty years or so. Just think, if you don't use it for a week, it costs not one penny in hay or grain." Mrs. Tanner made a face like a horse chewing oats and Alexia giggled.

"Nor does it fill a corral with manure," Mrs. Tanner went on. "It would be like having a cable car of one's own. Even better. It would go wherever you pointed it, not just follow the slot around the streets."

As if in answer to Mrs. Tanner, a cable car bell jangled up ahead of them. Alexia saw it go past, a red flash of color and clanging. For a second Alexia imagined having money of her own, to spend on whatever she wanted. She pictured herself in her lovely waist and gored skirt, dripping lace and confidence, seated in an automobile on her way to the opera. She laughed aloud.

"What are you thinking about?" Mrs. Tanner asked, her eyes twinkling. "Not automobiles, if the thoughts make you laugh like that."

Alexia shrugged. "In a way, I was." She described the daydream.

Mrs. Tanner winked approvingly. "Now picture yourself *driving* the thing."

Alexia shook her head. "Driving?"

Mrs. Tanner's eyes widened. "Some women do. And they say there's nothing to it that anyone of normal intelligence can't master in a few days' time."

Alexia stared in disbelief.

"Women drive carriages and freight teams, don't they?" Mrs. Tanner challenged her.

Alexia nodded. "Not often, though."

Mrs. Tanner laughed again. "But they do and they are perfectly able. And no automobile was ever harder to handle than a spirited horse. How could it be?"

They turned onto Market Street and Alexia hurried to keep up, staring up the thoroughfare at the huge buildings on either side of the street. She loved Market Street's smooth stone buildings rising up out of the earth so abruptly. Everything was elegant—even the crowds here were well dressed.

The men's dark suits and hats accented the colorful, ornate dresses of their wives and daughters. Alexia let Mrs. Tanner get a step or two ahead as they threaded their way through the people on the sidewalk. She looked up at the Spreckles Building. Next to it was the Parrot Building, squat, heavy, looking impossibly strong.

Alexia followed Mrs. Tanner across the Fifth Street intersection. There was a group of students milling around in front of the Academy of Sciences. The crowds made it hard to see the Mint across the street, and Alexia was disappointed.

Mrs. Tanner looked back from time to time, smiling. Alexia hurried a little to catch up. They crossed Fourth Street together, stepping back up onto the high curb almost in unison. Just ahead, the Call Building loomed, rising high enough to earn the name skyscraper. It always made Alexia feel small. She looked at the clock on the tower. It was nine thirty.

Alexia bumped into someone and apologized, embarrassed to have been looking at buildings instead of the sidewalk in front of her.

"Perfectly all right, miss," the young man said, looking down into her face. "Are you lost?"

"Oh, no, I'm just clumsy," Alexia said, blushing again. "I wasn't watching where I was going."

The man smiled, then touched his hat brim as he went on down the sidewalk. Alexia glanced back at him once, then turned to trot after Mrs. Tanner. As she turned her eyes swept across the crowds on the far side of the street. She caught her breath and stumbled to a stop, trying to see into the shadows beneath the awnings on the far side of Market Street.

"Alexia?"

Mrs. Tanner was walking back toward her. Alexia shrugged apologetically, then looked back across the street. She couldn't see him now, but she was almost sure that she had caught a glimpse of her father.

"What did you see?" Mrs. Tanner asked gently.

Alexia shook her head. "I bumped into someone, that's all."

Mrs. Tanner was watching her closely.

"I was looking up at the Call Building clock," Alexia added. "That's why I ran into him."

Mrs. Tanner winked. "We'll have to break you of that before you learn to drive an auto," she said somberly.

Alexia couldn't help but smile. They set off together again. This time, Mrs. Tanner stayed closer for the first half block or so. Once she was walking a little ahead again, Alexia stole a glance backward. It had been her father, she was pretty sure. But what was he doing up here on Market Street?

CHAPTER FIVE

As they came close to the Palace Hotel, Mrs. Tanner slowed her step. Alexia knew why. The Palace was one of the finest hotels in the world. It was famous for its hydraulic elevators, its fountains, and white marble baths—everything about it was absolutely first class.

Mrs. Tanner was always on the lookout for women who had just gotten back from France or England—or even New York. Their toilettes were often just a little ahead of the San Francisco trend. Mrs. Tanner often picked up some little flourish, some subtle touch in the designs that she could incorporate into her own work.

"Look at that one," Mrs. Tanner whispered, coming to a halt on the sidewalk directly across from the arched carriage court entry of the Palace.

Alexia looked across the street. A woman dressed in smoldering red was alighting from a carriage with a dark-suited gentleman. She was young and pretty, and her waist had been laced in so tightly that the upper part of her body resembled a flower on a slender stem. She was a living example of the Grecian bend, walking with tiny steps and the grace of a dancer, her torso arched back, her shoulders level, her chin high.

"What a lovely cut," Mrs. Tanner breathed. "Look at the drape those plaits in back give the skirt. Low like that, they give a whole different line."

Alexia stepped back to let the crowd pass, moving to stand next to Mrs. Tanner. The woman's hat was a riot of dyed red ostrich plumes that moved like exotic sea creatures in a rising tide as she laughed at her companion's remarks.

"You see," Mrs. Tanner said, half turning so that Alexia could hear her. "All the drawings and little dolls and photographs we get from Europe and England can't match being able to see a new style like this."

"She is beautiful," Alexia breathed. The woman was like a princess, a pampered lady from a fairy tale. Even the carriage was wonderful, with polished brass fittings on the harness, the horses a matched pair of bays.

"The bodice is cut an inch or so longer than the last batch of patterns I got from François." Mrs. Tanner was squinting a little, professionally analyzing the shape of the woman's dress.

Alexia knew that Mrs. Tanner and every other modiste in the city vied to make better fabric supplier contacts, to keep their acquaintances in Europe happy. Letters, packages, and crates were shipped to America every day. They brought cloth and trim, elaborate braids and laces—and, most important of all, drawings and patterns. If a modiste was not always on the edge of each trend, many of her clients would go elsewhere.

Alexia stared at the woman in red. Another, older woman, dressed in an elaborate toilette of dark green moiré silk, appeared on the sidewalk. She looked both ways, as if waiting for someone to escort her.

"Oh, dear!" Mrs. Tanner exclaimed suddenly.

Alexia whirled. Mrs. Tanner was lying on the sidewalk, an expression of pain on her face. A big man, obviously embarrassed and distressed, was standing over her.

"I am truly sorry, ma'am. I surely am." His

broad, florid face was absolutely sincere and his voice was rough and gravely. He reached down to take Mrs. Tanner's hand to pull her back to her feet. Mrs. Tanner jerked her hand away, grimacing.

"Please don't touch my hands," Mrs. Tanner told the man. "They are arthritic." Then she turned to Alexia. "I seem to have hurt my ankle," she said, and Alexia was amazed at the steadiness in her voice. It seemed out of place with the deep furrows of pain that marked her forehead.

"I'll help her," Alexia said quickly, moving around to squat close to Mrs. Tanner.

"Just let me straighten my skirts," Mrs. Tanner said in a hoarse whisper. She fought to sit up, plucking at her skirts to keep them around her ankles where they belonged. Alexia knew the unyielding metal busk of her corset made it almost impossible for her to bend forward at the waist.

Mrs. Tanner finally managed to get her feet beneath her and rose unsteadily. As she struggled to her feet Alexia took her right arm and the big man supported her left. Mrs. Tanner was gasping for a few seconds, fighting for each breath.

"Damnation and brimstone upon this ridiculous corset," Mrs. Tanner whispered. Alexia looked aside to hide her shock at Mrs. Tanner's improper language.

"Are you all right now, ma'am?" the red-faced man inquired politely.

Mrs. Tanner nodded. "I am. And I thank you for helping me up."

"If there is a thanks due, it isn't to me," he said in a courtly manner that made Alexia think of her father. He touched his hat and gave Mrs. Tanner a little bow. "You hardly need thank the one who knocked you down." He was looking earnestly into Mrs. Tanner's face, his eyes full of concern. "I hate to leave you without knowing that you are entirely safe," he added.

"I am that, I assure you," Mrs. Tanner said quickly. "Any help I need, Alexia can easily provide. I am not ill, sir."

"Your hands?" the man asked. "Are your hands all right?"

Mrs. Tanner glanced down at her hands, as if the question surprised her. Her swollen red knuckles stood out even more sharply than usual, Alexia noticed, and the back of her right hand looked scraped. The sidewalk had probably rubbed her skin raw when she had reached out to try to break her fall.

The man straightened his hat. "I thought you said you had hurt yourself."

Mrs. Tanner blushed. She hated attention

called to her arthritis. "My hands are fine, thank you—" she began, then stopped and took a deep breath. "I thought I had hurt my ankle."

The man stood silently, gazing at Mrs. Tanner. She seemed flustered. As Alexia watched, he bent close to whisper something near Mrs. Tanner's ear.

Mrs. Tanner made a sweeping motion with one hand. "No, no. Thank you, sir. My house is a long way from here, and we have an errand to complete before we start home. But I do thank you for your concern."

It finally dawned on Alexia that the man was hoping Mrs. Tanner would enlist his aid in some way. He kept offering her his arm as though he was convinced she needed to lean on something to remain upright. Alexia resisted an impulse to explain that Mrs. Tanner would have to have a broken leg before she was reduced to leaning on anyone. Even on days when her hands hurt so badly that it was hard to hold her scissors, she didn't ask for help.

The big man finally tipped his hat and turned to continue on down the sidewalk. He glanced back once or twice, then disappeared into the crowd. Alexia looked across the street. The young woman in red was gone.

"I apologize for my language," Mrs. Tanner

said quietly as they began walking once again. "I do hate corsets and I have never understood why proper women have to wear them. I wonder what would have become of me if I had fallen in front of a galloping coach. I would have lain there, a turtle on its back, until the wheels flattened me."

She said it with such fierce seriousness that Alexia smiled.

Mrs. Tanner shook her head and smiled back. "That fellow was watching our princess in red, too, I think. He walked into me as though I were an open door he was trying to hurry through. I don't think he ever saw me at all."

"He would have walked you home if you had given him the slightest encouragement," Alexia said. "Or he might have a carriage to offer. He liked you. I could tell."

Mrs. Tanner shook her head. "I don't think so. I think he simply felt bad that he knocked me over like that."

Alexia arched her brows. "I think he found you attractive. Would you ever consider remarrying?"

"Never," Mrs. Tanner said. "I was married to the best man on earth and I have no need of another marriage." She didn't give Alexia time to respond.

Mrs. Tanner went on more slowly than her usual stride. After half a block, when they were weaving through another thick crowd in front of the Grand Hotel, Alexia noticed an unevenness in her step.

"Your ankle is hurt, isn't it?"

"A little."

"We should start back now, then," Alexia said.

Mrs. Tanner brushed away her words with a quick motion of one hand. "Not until we have done what we came to do. If it hurts too much on the way home, perhaps we will have to take a cable car down to Seventh."

"That would be a terrible shame," Alexia said with mock sadness.

"You are a spoiled child," Mrs. Tanner teased back. "Do you imagine that I am made of money?"

"I thought you were!" Alexia pretended to be astonished.

A carriage rattled past, followed by a freight wagon filled with peaches. There were so many canneries in this part of the city that wagonloads of fruit were a common sight in late summer. The sweet odor of the fruit made Alexia close her eyes for an instant. "The smell of peaches makes me think of my mother," she said.

"Did she put up peaches?" Mrs. Tanner asked, as though it had been a perfectly normal comment for anyone to make about a wagonload of peaches on their way to a cannery.

Alexia nodded. "In big glass jars. And preserves, too."

Mrs. Tanner smiled. "How lovely that you have such nice memories of her."

Another wagonload of peaches went past and Alexia pretended to be overcome with the alluring odor that billowed out behind it.

Mrs. Tanner laughed aloud. "See that you don't fall off the curb." Her eyes were twinkling as she pulled Alexia toward her on the sidewalk.

Alexia turned to watch the fruit wagon disappear into the rolling parade of carts and coaches that surrounded the Palace Hotel. Closer to them, the Grand had its own set of delivery wagons pulling into the service drives.

"The big hotels are like small cities," Mrs. Tanner said, following her gaze. "They bring in everything for the guests—the deliveries start before dawn every morning. Tetrazzini stays at the Palace when she is here. So does the great Caruso."

Alexia heard the rapture in Mrs. Tanner's voice. "Have you heard him sing?"

Mrs. Tanner nodded. "Twice. And I will never forget a single moment of either occasion."

Alexia looked back at the Palace once more as they crossed Third Street and turned down it, walking even more slowly. Alexia could tell that Mrs. Tanner's ankle was bothering her.

Mrs. Tanner stepped around a couple shepherding four or five small children along the sidewalk. The littlest boy, still wearing his baby skirts, toddled along between two of his sisters. Alexia started around them, following Mrs. Tanner, then had to stop when the little boy fell, pulling one of his sisters down with him. Mrs. Tanner didn't glance back and kept going.

Once the children were on their feet again and had passed, Alexia hurried to catch up with Mrs. Tanner. Carriage after carriage was rolling down Market Street and they had to stop to let four or five go past before they could continue. As they began walking again, a cable car came clanging through the intersection. They stopped again to let it pass. Mrs. Tanner glanced at it, frowning. Alexia watched her sidelong as she took her next few steps across the tracks. The unevenness was still there.

Behind them, an auto roared up the street, slowing to a stop in front of the Grand Hotel. A cart horse pulling a load of firewood snorted and reared as it went by. The delivery boy shouted at the auto driver, shaking his fist as boxes in the back of his wagon slewed from one side to the other.

The automobile swerved and went on, passing

Alexia only a few feet away. The motorist wore goggles and a thick, long scarf. His suit looked like hunting garb, a sturdy light brown twilled cloth. There was a woman in the auto with him. She wore a huge hat, pinned on her head by a slender scarf of chiffon that tied solidly beneath her chin. Alexia wondered if she had ever driven the automobile herself. The idea of careening along, steering, made Alexia shiver.

Alexia glanced at Mrs. Tanner to find her smiling. "You would make a superb driver, Alexia."

Alexia smiled and shook her head. "How do you read my thoughts so often?"

Mrs. Tanner reached out and touched her forehead. "They appear like billboards upon your face. I, too, would love to learn to operate an automobile," Mrs. Tanner whispered like a conspirator. "Perhaps we will both do it one day."

They turned onto Kearny Street and got back up on the sidewalk. Alexia heard someone ahead of them shouting and took a few tiptoe strides, trying to see over the heads of the crowds heading toward Union Square. There was a wagon standing crisscross in the street. Two men were squared off, shouting. The language was not English.

"A right-of-way dispute perhaps," Mrs. Tanner said dryly. Ahead of them on the sidewalk, the foot traffic was slowing. People were staring at the argument—some of them stopped to watch.

Alexia rose back up on her toes, stretching up to see better. The two men looked furious, and as Alexia watched and listened, she realized that not only were they speaking a language other than English, they weren't speaking the *same* language. She could see heavy wooden tubs scattered on the street—they looked like butter tubs. Alexia glanced at Mrs. Tanner and got a wink.

"It could last a while at this rate, Alexia. Perhaps we should cross the street and avoid the crush."

They stepped off the high sidewalk and made their way carefully. Alexia skirted a pile of horse manure, guiding Mrs. Tanner around it. Then they both lifted their skirts a little to clear the pavement, trying not to dirty their hems. Mrs. Tanner bobbled once, and Alexia caught at her arm, steadying her as she navigated around a pothole.

"Thank you," Mrs. Tanner said politely. Her voice sounded tight and strained.

Alexia stopped behind two tall men in black coats, then started forward again when they did. She wished the crowd would thin. It seemed as though every person on this end of Market Street had suddenly appeared to watch the argument.

Alexia saw Mrs. Tanner wince on her next step. "How is your ankle?"

"An annoyance. No more than that." Mrs. Tanner's head was high, her shoulders squared.

As they stepped up onto the sidewalk on the far side of the street, Alexia breathed a sigh of relief. Here, at least, there would be fewer potholes and no manure. She glanced back along the sidewalk and caught her breath in astonishment—nearly losing her own footing. A second later the crowd shifted and she wasn't sure whether she had imagined it—or if her eyes had been telling her the truth.

"Whatever is wrong?" Mrs. Tanner asked. "You haven't twisted *your* ankle, have you?"

"Nothing is wrong," Alexia answered as calmly as she could. "I just stumbled a little, that's all."

Mrs. Tanner was studying her face. "You're pale, Alexia. Do you feel well?"

"I am worried about you walking this far," Alexia answered, and her voice was smooth and normal again. She inhaled slowly. "We shouldn't walk up to Robinson's."

Mrs. Tanner frowned as she led the way around the next corner, turning left up Myrtle Street. "We probably had better not. I hate to miss the parrots, but I must admit my ankle does hurt a little more now."

Alexia risked a glanced backward. The faces behind them were all strangers now, but she was almost certain that she had seen her father again. He had been talking to a man with a long drooping mustache—and the man who had accidently knocked Mrs. Tanner down.

Alexia swallowed, resisting her desire to look back again. It made no sense at all. Maybe she had been mistaken. Why would her father be talking to the florid-faced man? Did they somehow know each other? Why would they?

Alexia felt Mrs. Tanner looking at her again, so she scanned the crowd coming toward them as they entered Union Square. "Look at that green velvet waist," she breathed, gesturing at a woman walking toward them. A green lace inset covered her throat and décolleté, but the cloth was puckered around her sleeve scye, ruining the line of the waist.

"Terrible fit," Mrs. Tanner agreed. "She should have come to us."

"She should have come to *you*," Alexia answered, laughing, trying to sound as though nothing out of the ordinary was happening. Maybe it wasn't. She was so worried about her father it was possible she had just seen someone who looked like him standing near the red-faced man—and had imagined the rest.

It was certainly possible. Of course it was. Alexia tried to convince herself as they walked on.

CHAPTER SIX

The White House department store was crowded. Women filed into the elevator around them, a close-packed sea of perfume and lace. One of them wore bloomers, Alexia saw, and a loose waist with a sailor's collar. Some of the other women gave her sidelong glances as the iron gate doors closed and the elevator began to move. Mrs. Tanner kept her eyes fixed on the ornate iron.

They got off on the third floor. Mrs. Tanner led the way as usual. Even with her throbbing ankle, she took long steps and knew exactly where she was headed.

The cabinets were side by side along a back

wall, the dark oak and glass polished to a high sheen. Threads were displayed along shallow shelves, one color beside the next in the rainbow, lightest colors on the middle shelves where everyone could see them.

"You are going to need new frillies to go with your new dress," Mrs. Tanner said as she held up the slender piece of plum silk to compare colors. "At least drawers and a corset cover. Maybe a chemise—and petticoats."

Alexia answered, but she wasn't sure what she had said even a few seconds after she had said it. Her mind was spinning with uneasy thoughts about her father. She kept picturing him, standing on Market Street, saying something to the florid-faced man, then glancing in both directions like a thief. What had he been doing?

"This is the closest, don't you think?"

Alexia looked at the spool of thread Mrs. Tanner was pointing at. It wasn't quite right. But the other purples were bluer still. "That's pretty close," she said.

"I could have ordered thread dyed to match, but I think this will do nicely, and it will save Miss Helm a little money."

"Does she need to save money?" Alexia asked, trying to make a joke.

Mrs. Tanner looked at her for a few seconds before she answered. "Of course. Everyone needs to save money."

"Not the Rothschilds, or the Hearsts, or—"

"Thrift is a virtue."

"But a few cents wouldn't make any difference to someone who—"

"But if I can save her a few pennies without compromising the quality of the garment, I will. Because I hate waste, I suppose," Mrs. Tanner said.

Alexia looked back at the threads. There was one reddish purple on the shelf above. It had been set beside the scarlets and carmines, but it was purple—the perfect red-plum color. She pointed and the hovering salesclerk behind the counter plucked down a wooden spool and held it so that Mrs. Tanner could see.

"That one is much better, Alexia. Good for you!"

Mrs. Tanner's voice was so full of warmth that Alexia felt a little guilty. "I was just lucky enough to see it. I didn't really do anything."

"You kept looking once I had quit. That's more than luck."

Two women near them glanced over and Alexia turned away.

"You underestimate yourself, Alexia," Mrs.

Tanner went right on. "Few girls your age could do as well with such complicated sewing as you have done. You have a real gift for it. I was looking at your work this morning on the bodice. I think you should consider entering the trade."

Alexia looked up, her discomfort fading beneath a surge of delight. "Really? You do?"

Mrs. Tanner winked. "I do. But only if you are willing to work," she added, her voice serious.

Alexia looked aside, a feeling of joy rising inside her. It was so strong that it was unsettling. A modiste. She had never thought about trying to *be* anything.

"Pink would go well beneath your silk," Mrs. Tanner was saying.

Alexia looked up at her. It was a few seconds before her words sank in, and even then the wonderful feeling was still there, nestled in the pit of Alexia's stomach. A modiste! She imagined herself in her own little shop, her own shears and tools laid out neatly. If she had a shop, she could live above it just as Mrs. Tanner did. And she would never move. She would build up a clientele and they would employ her, and she would fix up her apartment a little more each year until it was beautiful.

"For your underskirt, Alexia?" Mrs. Tanner said

very distinctly, and Alexia knew she had missed something.

She stared at Mrs. Tanner. "The underskirt?"

Mrs. Tanner laughed. "Your thoughts are certainly elsewhere, aren't they? Petticoats beneath with lace, of course, but something a little pinker than the color of the silk on the underskirt. But just a touch of it. Look at this braid." She tapped the glass front of a cabinet and the salesclerk took out a spool of braid for her to examine.

Alexia pulled out her bit of fabric and Mrs. Tanner laid the braid atop it. It was beautiful, the satin cords looped and woven in a delicate pattern.

"It would work very well," Mrs. Tanner said. "Do you like it?"

Alexia nodded cautiously. She had no money to buy garniture of any kind—certainly not lovely silk braid like this. "I shall speak to my father and perhaps someday—"

"—I was thinking more along the lines of a bargain," Mrs. Tanner said. "Between you and me."

Alexia met her eyes. "A bargain?"

"Yes." Mrs. Tanner was using her serious business voice. Alexia recognized it instantly. It was the tone she took when she was discussing cost with her clients. "I will purchase this braid now. But I would like you to help out in the kitchen a bit, serving and clearing mostly. Maybe a little more if Cook needs extra help. Only until school begins. Say, two hours a day, in addition to working with me in the shop. Can you do that?"

Alexia touched the satiny surface of the braid. "Of course." Then, Alexia's fingers froze on the braid. "We should apply anything I make to the rent past due," she said slowly. "Not to fancy braid for my skirt. I already owe you a great favor for the silk and all your hours teaching me, and I . . ." Alexia trailed off, her eyes stinging.

"I will handle this business of rent with your father, Alexia," Mrs. Tanner said. "This is a separate agreement, between us, as friends. Cook needs help serving and organizing. I am slow at it." She rubbed her hands together and Alexia glanced at them. Mrs. Tanner frowned and looked aside. "Too often everything is cooled by the time we begin eating," she finished.

Alexia nodded slowly, sorry she had made Mrs. Tanner self-conscious about her hands. She took a deep breath and handed the braid back to the clerk. "I'll work in the kitchen and you tally whatever I earn. If it isn't needed for rent, I'll bargain it for the braid. But if it is needed—"

"An admirable solution, Alexia," Mrs. Tanner said. Her voice was soft, almost sad. "We should be getting back, I think. My ankle is throbbing like an extra heartbeat."

"I had forgotten completely," Alexia admitted.

Alexia followed Mrs. Tanner through the bolts of velvet and linen, trailing her fingers across the cloth as she walked. There was heavy wool cravenette for coats and cloaks and jackets—and gossamer crepeline in so many colors that Alexia felt as if she were walking through a flower garden.

The bargain ribbon table was covered in flat spools made of heavy brown paper. The White House had a wonderful selection of silk moiré and watered taffetas. There were thin grosgrain baby ribbons and wide velvets of every color. The velvets were on special sale today. There was a notice taped to the edge of the table. Alexia read it: *Today only, ten yards of Number four, any color, ten cents.*

"You need hooks and eyes," Mrs. Tanner explained, veering off to a set of shallow bins set against the far wall. "For your waist, I think these will be good." She extended her hand and Alexia saw a little mound of tiny steel eyelets, each one a perfect clover-shaped loop of slender steel wire.

Alexia stared at them. "They're so tiny."

"You are growing up. You can fasten these perfectly well. And these will disappear, almost, and that is precisely the effect you want."

Alexia nodded. "I will ask my—"

"These will amount to less than a few pennies, Alexia," Mrs. Tanner interrupted her. "And you cannot finish the waist without them. Call it an early birthday gift."

Alexia stiffened, hoping the next question wouldn't come, but, of course, it did.

"When is your birthday, Alexia? We have never celebrated it at the lodging house, have we? Haven't you been here a year?"

Mrs. Tanner looked genuinely puzzled and Alexia swallowed, wondering if she should just fib and be done with it. But she hadn't ever lied to Mrs. Tanner about anything except her father, and she didn't want to start now. "My father thinks it's the fourth of July. That's what he says, anyway. But he forgets most years, so I don't make a fuss," she added when she saw Mrs. Tanner's mouth tighten.

"He *thinks* it's the fourth?"

Alexia nodded. "He wasn't there when I was born and he isn't sure. My mother always celebrated it—he knows it was in the summer and—"

"Where was he?" Mrs. Tanner was searching her eyes and it made Alexia so uneasy that she half turned, pretending to look at a woman in a sweeping blue dress.

"He was traveling and he had some trouble

and couldn't make it back in time. My aunt was with my mother. She wasn't alone."

"I am glad to hear that," Mrs. Tanner said. She was still holding the hooks and eyes. "Let's pay for these. I want to start home."

Alexia followed her to the cash clerk. Mrs. Tanner stood quietly while the woman totted it up. The thread came to fifty cents, and Alexia heard Mrs. Tanner take in a quick sharp breath. "I can get Eureka silk thread through the Sears, Roebuck catalogue for forty-five cents a dozen spools."

Alexia saw that the salesclerk was not discomfited. "Yes, you can, ma'am," she said. "But it is so hard to get the color needed that way."

Alexia knew this was true. Mrs. Tanner had said it herself. Black or white thread was easy to mail order. Colors were harder. They might try to have standard names, but every manufacturer dyed slightly differently.

"We have some lovely dress shields on sale," the clerk said, undaunted by the ire in Mrs. Tanner's expression.

Mrs. Tanner shook her head. "I have no need of dress shields today, thank you."

Alexia pressed her arms against her sides. Her own dress shields were tattered and the absorbent padding was flattened with wear. Before she wore her new dress, she would have to buy a new pair. It would be foolish to spend dozens of hours sewing, then ruin the dress with a single day's perspiration.

Alexia felt a little flutter of unhappiness inside. Why did everything have to depend on money? The need seemed endless. Maybe she would marry well, as her father always said. Or maybe she could be a modiste. The flutter subsided.

Mrs. Tanner opened her purse and took out the coins. She counted them out slowly, placing each one in the clerk's hand. Then she turned and led the way back to the elevator.

On the way down, there were fewer people. Alexia was glad. When the little iron gates shut, she closed her eyes for a few seconds, trying to bring back the wonderful daydream of being a modiste one day. But the elevator stopped with a little jolt and she opened her eyes.

CHAPTER SEVEN

Market Street was still crowded as they came around the Third Street corner and saw the arched entrances and the lines of carriages.

The two men who had been arguing in the street had gone, at least. The crowds were moving in an orderly fashion now.

Mrs. Tanner's limp was quite noticeable now. Her face was set in a grim expression as she walked. Cable cars clanged past every five or six minutes, but she ignored them. She walked in silence and Alexia wasn't sure whether or not she wanted conversation—so she stayed quiet, too.

Walking this side of Market, they passed the

Mint, with its lawns and fountains and beautiful stone pillars—and this time Alexia could see. She never tired of looking at the polished stone. Her father called the Mint the entrance to paradise. Alexia knew he meant the building was beautiful, but she knew he meant more than that, too. Money again. Was it always the key to everything?

As they turned toward Third Street, Alexia saw Mrs. Tanner's eyes stray ahead a few blocks, to the little row of groceries. Two of them were owned by one big Italian family. The third was owned by a rival—a small, soft-spoken widower from Sicily. They kept each other's prices down with an ongoing, fierce competition. Mrs. Tanner would rarely buy groceries anywhere else.

"I need to order some things," Mrs. Tanner said, wincing a little as the uneven sidewalk made her ankle flex.

"I can come do it after dinner," Alexia offered.

Mrs. Tanner looked at her gratefully. "If your father has no objection, that would be a great help. I will make you out a list. You can be back long before dark."

Alexia nodded. Her father forbade her to walk outside after dark. After nightfall the saloons along Howard Street were too rowdy—there were too many transient men without families or even friends to keep them busy and out of trouble.

As they turned slowly up Howard Street, Mrs. Tanner gestured up the block. "Go to the Galleno brother in the middle store—where we usually go. His produce is the best, and he always gives me a free head of cabbage with every corned beef I buy from him. His butter is good, too. Sweet and fresh. And, the truth is, I just like to chat with him."

Alexia nodded, feeling a rumble in her stomach at so much talk about food. Mrs. Tanner walked stolidly along Howard Street, lapsing back into silence. Alexia kept glancing at Mrs. Tanner. Her limp was getting worse.

When they finally passed the last of the big boarding hotels and rounded the corner onto Langton, Mrs. Tanner handed Alexia the shop keys and motioned for her to run ahead to unlock the door.

Mrs. Tanner put the thread and the little bag of hooks and eyes in the shop. Coming out, she arched her brows. "May we start our new arrangement today? Cook has an elaborate meal planned and I know she would appreciate help."

Alexia smiled. She had been hoping Mrs. Tanner would want her to start immediately.

"Go up and wash, then, and rest a few minutes," Mrs. Tanner suggested.

Alexia nodded. She went into the downstairs parlor just behind Mrs. Tanner. The stairs weren't long or steep and Alexia was glad for Mrs. Tanner's sake. She went up them like a toddler, stepping up with her uninjured right foot first, then bringing her left up to meet it. With a little wave, she turned into her apartment at the top of the stairs.

Alexia went on across the reception room to her door. The glass knob felt cool to her touch as she turned it. Inside, everything seemed small and cramped—and unfamiliar in some strange way. The shabby bedstead and the little beat-up chest of drawers seemed even older and more scarred today than usual. The chest of drawers hadn't been at the Market Street auction, Alexia admitted to herself. It had belonged to an Irish family with ten children. Her father had won it in a card game.

Alexia hesitated in the center of the room, then decided just to wash her face and hands. Right before dinner the washroom was often occupied— sometimes a little line formed.

The wash basin had enough clean water in it to splash her face with clear water, then to rinse her hands. Alexia turned once she had finished and faced the room again.

She went to stand beside her mother's trunk, pressing her palms flat against the smooth arched lid for a few seconds. Then she lay down carefully on the bed, flat on her back so her corset wouldn't dig into her skin. She closed her eyes and tried not to think about her father or the rent, or anything else.

"Alexia? Are you ready to come down now?" Mrs. Tanner tapped on the door a little while later. "Are you rested, Alexia?"

Alexia went to open the door. "I was waiting for Papa to get back."

"He was just downstairs. He has had an offer of some kind of a position," Mrs. Tanner said, her eyes sparkling. "It sounds like quite a wonderful opportunity. He begins in the morning."

Alexia hesitated, letting her eyes slide from Mrs. Tanner's face. Her father might easily be fibbing about a new position. If he was, Alexia knew, she would end up having to conceal the truth, too. Alexia sighed. She didn't want to tell lies to Mrs. Tanner—not even small ones.

"I do believe our wonderful Cook has something quite special in the works this noon," Mrs. Tanner said. "Amy is such a treasure. She got a handful of receipts through a friend who works at the Palace."

Alexia wished her father hadn't told Mrs. Tanner he already had a new position. She was so nice, so straightforward—she would probably never even suspect he would lie about something like that.

Alexia could only hope that she was wrong—or that her father would soon have a real position, and then it wouldn't matter what he'd said. Maybe it was true. Maybe that was what he had been doing up on Market Street earlier. Alexia felt her heart rise a little. She came out of the door and closed it, then walked with Mrs. Tanner to the head of the stairs.

"Did you hear me?" Mrs. Tanner asked, pausing. "I said Cook got receipts from the Palace Hotel."

Alexia mustered a smile. "The Palace? I thought only famous people and rich financiers got to eat that sort of food."

"Well, normally, that's the case," Mrs. Tanner agreed, laughing softly. "Now, mind you, Cook says we are using Chinatown chicken rather than fancy imported English pheasant, of course, but beyond that, all else is identical." Mrs. Tanner went down the first three steps, easing her weight carefully from her sound ankle to the one she had twisted. "Identical," she repeated and giggled.

Halfway down the staircase, Mrs. Tanner paused again and turned, talking from one side of her mouth. "Well, if you insist on complete accuracy, the fine old wine the Palace chef uses in the sauce is imported from France and ours was made here in California last month. Our asparagus is local as well—from one of the Galleno brothers on Third Street. And I suppose"—she trailed her hand along the bannister like a socialite gliding her way into a ballroom—"I suppose our flatware can hardly compare with their silver and crystal. And we have no chandelier, nor a staff of eager and silent servants in starched white uniforms for each diner . . . but—" She paused dramatically and Alexia took her cue.

"Beyond that, every other detail is identical?"

"Precisely," Mrs. Tanner said. "Oh, by the way, Alexia," she said as she opened the door into the dining room. "Remember as you set the table that Mr. Chair won't be here this noon. He's off on another trip. He seems to do so well at selling those clumsy-looking shoes of his."

"He's showed them to me," Alexia said, nodding. "They're work boots for farmers and miners, I guess."

"Your father will be back," Mrs. Tanner said quietly as they got to the bottom of the stairs. "He said something about a quick glass of beer to celebrate his good fortune. He said he would be here in time to eat with us."

Alexia sighed. Of course. Papa would have hurried down to the Corona House saloon for his nickel beer if he had quit the print shop and had the rest of the day off.

Alexia heard the side yard door open and turned, but it wasn't her father. It was one of the twins. Whichever one this one was, she was smiling cordially.

"Hello, Mrs. Tanner. Good afternoon, Alexia."

Alexia took in a deep breath, staring at the white hair, the perfect costume. "Hello, Miss . . ." she trailed off, pretending to cough.

"No one can, or ever could, tell us apart, you know," the twin said. From her annoyed tone Alexia knew it was Miss Harvest, but she didn't dare interrupt.

"Even when we were little," Miss Harvest went on. "We had blond hair then, long, in ringlets down our backs. Mother would never let anyone cut it, even though it cost her hours with the brush and comb to keep the tangles from taking over. Long hair was all the style back then and—"

"—I doubt if either one of them give two cents or a tinker's hoot about how long our hair was when we were babes, Harvest."

Alexia turned to see Miss Pleasant coming in behind her sister. They wore identical dresses.

Alexia knew as soon as she went into the kitchen and came out again she would lose track of which was which.

"Of course we are interested in your memories of your childhood," Mrs. Tanner was saying graciously. "I always find Miss Harvest's memories of Boston compelling."

Alexia nodded, seeing the expression of ruffled dignity on Miss Harvest's face. "I do, too," she said, trying to look sincere.

Miss Pleasant laughed again, a silvery sound, like notes from a music box. "You are both far too kind."

"We are having quite a special meal this afternoon," Mrs. Tanner said. Miss Pleasant and Miss Harvest both turned their attention to her.

Alexia skipped downstairs as the women talked. She crossed the long, narrow parlor, allowing herself one quick glance at the beautiful piano that stood in the far end of the room, settled firmly on an Oriental carpet of deep blue and amber. Then she pushed open the door to the dining room and crossed it in four or five long strides. She went into the kitchen.

The windows were clouded white with steam. The cookstove stood against the back wall, its clean, well-blackened chimney pipe running halfway to the ceiling, then turning to go out through the wall. It was a very modern Glenwood range, the lettering on its oven doors clear on the clean white enamel. This time of year, Cook used the gas half of the range. In the winter, she used coal in the firebox to heat the kitchen and dining room while she cooked.

Today, two big pots stood close together right above the firebox. Alexia could see them vibrating as they boiled violently, their lids chattering. The white wall behind the range was scrubbed spotless.

"Ah, there you are," Cook said. Her name was Miss Amy Demerer, but Alexia had never heard anyone address her as anything but Cook—except Miss Tanner.

"Miss Tanner said you needed a bit of extra help?"

Cook nodded. "She told me you might start today. You can begin by setting the table, then I'll want you back in here, Miss Alexia." Her cheeks were webbed with tiny rose-colored veins—a result of leaning over hot stoves all of her life, Alexia's father had said. Alexia liked Cook's rosy face. It made her look cheerful and busy and a little out of breath all the time.

Alexia moved to the dish cupboard. This was modern, too, with a work shelf built into the cabinet front. Cook's ladles and serving utensils were laid out on the shelf. The Dunlop cream whip and the sugar sifter lay side by side.

Alexia counted out six plates, remembering to subtract Mr. Chair from the usual total of seven. Then she got the silver from its rosewood box. Even though she joked about it not being as fine as the Palace's, Mrs. Tanner had grown up in a well-to-do family and she still had a few beautiful things from her parents. This silver was from England.

"Will we need the milk pitcher?" Alexia asked.

Cook looked up from her pastry board where the biscuit dough lay in buttery crumbs next to her pastry cutter and her white marble rolling pin. "I think so. That wagoner boy, Cecil Straight, loves cool milk with every meal it seems." Expertly, she drizzled ice water over the dough, then mounded it and began to roll it out with quick, light strokes. "Mrs. Tanner used to try to slow him down. She won't care now that she gets plenty from that Swede who owes her money for his daughter's bridal trousseau." Cook shook her head. She turned the handle of the flour receptacle and half filled a cup measure. She began dusting her dough with it.

"I saw him yesterday and wondered who he was," Alexia said, wishing Cook would stop working to talk or stop talking to work. It was impossible to know if she was finished with a topic—or if she was just pausing to gather her thoughts.

As if to prove Alexia's point, Cook picked up her biscuit cutter and began punching out the little flattened rounds—plopping each one onto the baking sheet an inch or so from the last. Then, just as Alexia started to walk away, Cook started talking again. "All those frillies and nighties cost a great deal. He owns a dairy out in the western addition."

Cook fell back to work and Alexia hovered, hesitating. The instant she started to move away, Cook spoke once more.

"Fairly well-to-do, I'm told," Cook said. "You remember that big order of frillies. All linen and silk, not a nainsook among them. It's too much milk, though. We won't use it. No one really likes pudding or cottage cheese. I'll end up feeding it to the dogs down on Howard Street."

Alexia made a polite sound that she hoped would serve as a response and ducked out through the door, back into the dining room. The long table was made of dark wood, and it smelled of the lemon oil that Mrs. Tanner used to clean it. The tablecloth was embroidered linen, another relic of Mrs. Tanner's Philadelphia upbringing. They had talked about it once. Mrs. Tanner had lived in Chestnut Hill, a community of farmers Alexia had been to once with her father—in search of a man who owed him money from a wager. All Alexia remembered about Chestnut Hill was the huge trees lining the roads. Mrs. Tanner had been tickled that she remembered anything about it at all. Alexia laid the plates out, then began the silverware.

"Hello!" a hearty voice boomed out from the doorway, and Alexia looked up to see her father. He was smiling, his even white teeth showing from beneath his mustache. "And how fare you this beautiful day, my daughter?"

Alexia smiled at his comic formality. He seemed so happy. Maybe that meant good news. Maybe he really had found a new job.

CHAPTER EIGHT

Alexia stared into her father's handsome face, trying to read his eyes. He widened his smile and crossed the room. "How is Mrs. Tanner today?" he asked quietly.

Alexia shrugged. "What do you mean? She hurt her ankle walking and—"

"I mean her arthritis. Still bad?"

Alexia searched her father's face. "I suppose. Why do you ask?"

"No particular reason," her father said, reaching out to coax a stray strand of hair back from her forehead. "I am just concerned about her." His expression changed. "I'm sure she told you I have found a new position?"

Alexia swallowed and nodded.

"She really does meddle in our affairs too much," Alexia's father said, bending close to whisper. "I know how fond you are of her. But she isn't a good influence on you, Fairy Princess."

From the stairs Mrs. Tanner's voice mixed with the softer tones of the twins. A moment later they came into the room together. The twins wandered to the side door and went out to stand on the porch. Alexia could hear them discussing the dampness in the breeze.

Alexia's father had straightened up the instant he saw Mrs. Tanner. Now he was smiling. "The food smells wonderful, as always." His voice was warm and sincere.

Mrs. Tanner tilted her head to answer. "And you are always so very kind, Mr. Finsdale."

Alexia found herself glancing back and forth between them. What did he mean, Mrs. Tanner meddled? About what? Alexia watched her father hook his hands in his waistcoat pockets. "The oddest thing happened today," he began. Then he paused, like a child who has recited a riddle and is waiting for incorrect answers before he will tell the right one.

Alexia held her breath. Was he going to say he

had seen them on Market Street? Or that his friend had been the one to bump Mrs. Tanner? She said a silent chant that he would. Then everything would have a simple, innocent explanation.

"What?" Mrs. Tanner finally obliged him.

Alexia stood very still as her father widened his smile and shrugged. "I met a young woman today wearing a dress so perfectly fitted and beautifully made, I knew it was one of yours. So I took the liberty of asking if Mrs. A. H. Tanner was her modiste. The poor woman very nearly fainted. I suppose I am lucky that she didn't call for a policeman." Alexia watched her father laugh. "But then she softened when I told her I knew you and lived in your lodging house."

Mrs. Tanner smiled. "You were fortunate she believed you."

Alexia's father absently smoothed his mustache with one finger. "She said that you had made the dress nearly five years ago."

Alexia stared at her father. He was up to something, she just knew it. He was acting too friendly, overly polite—like he did when he was trying to take advantage of someone.

"Five years ago? Tell her I can easily replace the sleeves," Mrs. Tanner said. "It is likely time to refurbish the dress. Or if the whole waist is worn

I could fit her with a new bodice in a different fabric altogether."

"She said she was surprised you were still sewing," Alexia's father said quietly, as though he had just remembered the comment and had been puzzled by it. "I told her you had some difficult days but that usually you had no trouble at all."

Alexia deliberately set the silver down, piece by piece, unable to look at her father for a moment. What was he trying to do? He knew how much this would upset Mrs. Tanner. Alexia had told him how proud she was if people offered sympathy.

"Please do sit down, Mr. Finsdale," Mrs. Tanner was saying in a crisp tone. She gestured to his customary chair at the head of the table—opposite her own. Then she looked up as Cecil Straight came bounding through the dining room door.

Alexia liked Cecil. He was good-hearted and modest. He had red hair and more freckles than would fit across his nose. They overlapped, one running into the next. When he blushed, which was often, Cecil's freckles seemed to get a little darker.

"Good day, Mrs. Tanner," Cecil said breathlessly. "I am sorry to be late."

"You aren't," Mrs. Tanner assured him. "Cook is just finishing up the biscuits now. We will have time for a moment's more conversation before we eat."

As she spoke the twins came in from the side porch, closing the door behind them. Cecil sat down in his usual place. Pleasant and Harvest, as always, seemed not to know where to sit, then settled themselves beside Alexia's father. They always sat this way—but they would switch sides from time to time so it was impossible to be quite sure which was which even at the table.

"And how is your day at work turning out?" one of the twins asked Cecil. "You said at breakfast that there was a new foreman?" Alexia thought it was Miss Harvest speaking. The question seemed sterner than Miss Pleasant's usual conversation.

Cecil nodded. "He seems a decent enough fellow. I would not like to see him get angry. He's at least six feet tall, and heavy-built. Russian, I think. His name is Ivan. He seems to know horses well."

Alexia's father was nodding the whole time Cecil was talking. The instant there was silence, he leaned forward and addressed Cecil, his gaze intense. Alexia could only stare.

"Have you been hauling much flour up into Chinatown?"

Cecil shook his head. "Only to the white groceries up there. The Chinese don't have much use for the kind of flour the Bower's mill has for sale."

"They tend to use rice flour for their noodles and such, don't they?" This was the other twin and now Alexia was pretty sure she had them sorted out. Miss Pleasant often asked these kinds of questions that gave someone else an opportunity to speak, but really required no answer at all. She was sure of her facts, just trying to help the conversation along.

"I believe that's correct," Miss Harvest put in.

Mrs. Tanner was nodding. "Rice is like wheat to them. They use it for everything."

Alexia glanced around the table. Cecil and her father were staring into the air. Neither one cared enough about cooking to listen to discourse on Chinese flour.

"Alexia, perhaps you could help Cook carry out the food when she's ready."

Alexia ducked her head, embarrassed. She had been so busy listening that she had completely forgotten that she was supposed to be working. She turned toward the kitchen doors, mumbling an apology. Mrs. Tanner caught at her sleeve and winked. Alexia smiled at her, grateful that she was so kind.

Turning once more toward the kitchen doors, Alexia saw that her father was staring at her. He was frowning thoughtfully. She turned her head slightly, hoping that he wasn't going to say anything else to upset Mrs. Tanner.

Cook was taking golden brown biscuits from the oven. The asparagus steamed in its cream sauce. The baked chickens—there were three—sat atop the woodstove in agate-ware baking pans. Their breasts were honey brown. Sitting on the sideboard were sliced tomatoes and mashed potatoes. A gravy boat was filled, resting in a pan of hot water on the right side of the stove.

"Potatoes and tomatoes," Cook said brusquely.

Alexia picked up the potato bowl. It was pleasantly hot, the steam roiling upward as she walked. She set it in the center of the table on one of the thick quilted pads that Mrs. Tanner had made for this purpose.

"The railroads do have far too much influence," Mrs. Tanner was saying to Alexia's father.

He laughed, too loudly. "Influence? It seems to a lot of folks that they change any vote they want to change."

Alexia was going back through the doors before she could hear more of what they were saying, but politics were a bad subject—Mrs.

Tanner had very definite opinions and so did her father.

"I'll bring the meat platter," Cook said as Alexia came through the doorway.

Alexia nodded. As she picked up the asparagus and the plate of biscuits, Cook was lifting the roast chickens onto a serving platter, using broad-spooned tongs. Alexia went out the door, glancing anxiously toward her father as she crossed the room. He beamed at her.

"Alexia, Mrs. Tanner says you are becoming quite a seamstress. Why haven't you said anything about it to me?"

"I expect she wanted to surprise you," Mrs. Tanner said quickly, shooting Alexia an apologetic look.

Alexia smiled at Mrs. Tanner to let her know that she wasn't angry. After all, she had never told Mrs. Tanner she wanted to keep the dress a secret.

"Alexia?" her father repeated. "Why haven't you told me? I thought you were just sweeping up scraps and carrying bolts of cloth around when Mrs. Tanner had trouble with things because of her hands."

Alexia felt a terrible sense of danger. What was he doing? It was as though he just didn't care what Mrs. Tanner thought of him—of them. He should be especially careful to be polite to her now, when they owed back rent. He was fully aware of how much any mention of her arthritis upset Mrs. Tanner. Was he trying to anger her? Why? Something was terribly wrong.

CHAPTER NINE

"I'm not sure why I didn't tell you," Alexia managed, setting down the biscuits, sliding the plate toward Cecil so he could start eating.

She walked around the table to set the asparagus beside Miss Pleasant.

"Oh, this is lovely," she breathed.

"Indeed it is," Miss Harvest agreed bluntly. "Now, enough of your politics and shoptalk. We should all simply enjoy this meal."

At that moment Cook came in carrying the meat platter. A little chorus of *oh*s and *ah*s went around the table. Alexia risked a glance at her father. He was staring at her. She wished he would just fill his plate and eat. Warm food might lessen the effect the beer had had upon him.

Cook stood a moment, carving the fowl into steaming slices. Once she was finished, Mrs. Tanner took a portion, then lifted the platter to pass it on. It was heavy and Alexia could tell that it hurt her hands to pick it up.

Miss Harvest and Miss Pleasant served themselves gracefully, chattering about nothing. Alexia went back to the kitchen for the butter dish and glasses of water for everyone except Cecil. Alexia saw Perseus sneak in through the side porch door. He slid along the wall, past the table and into the kitchen. Cook always saved a few scraps for him, but he knew enough not to beg at the table.

The conversation had turned to President Roosevelt and talk of a great canal being dug across Panama. Alexia stole glances at her father as she came and went. He seemed to be enjoying himself immensely, soaking in every word that was said.

Cecil smiled broadly as Alexia set down his glass, then the milk pitcher, beside him. "Thank you," he said softly.

Alexia nodded to acknowledge his thanks. Cecil was twenty, she knew, but he looked much younger. The blushing didn't help.

Alexia went one more time to the kitchen. "Is there more I should do?" she asked Cook.

"No, no. You go ahead and join them now, Miss Alexia."

"You don't need to call me Miss," Alexia said, smiling. "I work here, same as you."

"I'll try," Cook promised. Alexia stood, looking around the kitchen. "Am I to help with cleanup?"

Cook shook her head. "I don't think so, dear. Perhaps tomorrow. Mrs. Tanner said something about you going up to the grocery for her."

"I forgot," Alexia said. "She asked me to do it when we were coming home."

"Her poor ankle is aching," Cook said somberly. "And it will be well nigh impossible to keep her off of it, I know."

Alexia smiled. "She is proud."

Cook laid her index finger beside her nose, glancing around before she leaned close to whisper. "Proud? She is *stubborn* is what she is. As stubborn as the day is long." She nodded knowingly, but Alexia could see her mouth twitching as she tried to fight off a smile. "That is not to say I am not very fond of her," she added, her voice still low.

"I am, too," Alexia whispered.

"You will never find a better chance," Cook said. "Learn all you can from her. She showed me your sewing the other morning. I could never do so well."

"Alexia?"

"Yes, Mrs. Tanner?" she answered, smiling at Cook to let her know she appreciated the praise.

"Your dinner will be stone cold if you dilly-dally any longer in there."

Alexia gave Cook another quick smile, then went through the door. She slid into her seat next to her father and settled into her chair, listening. The conversation was still centered on the canal Roosevelt wanted to dig across Panama. Everyone passed food to Alexia. Her father held the meat platter while she took her share of the roast chicken—but he kept talking.

"It's the malaria that's made it impossible so far," he said. His voice was a little too loud, but it seemed to Alexia that some of the boisterous effect of the beer had eased. She was grateful. Maybe they would get through the meal without him actually insulting Mrs. Tanner by discussing her infirmity when she clearly didn't wish to.

"I read an article in the *Chronicle*," Mrs. Tanner said quietly. "The reporter assured the public that the malaria is being brought under control. Roosevelt has a good man down there now, a Colonel Gorgas, as I recall—"

"It's more the yellow fever that causes the problems," Alexia's father interrupted her. His shoulders were squared and his voice had risen a little. He went on, recounting everything the newspapers had said about the canal, criticizing the way everything was being handled.

Alexia's hope for a peaceful meal fell apart. Mrs. Tanner was listening as Alexia's father talked. Miss Harvest was rapt, one hand beneath her chin, her food forgotten for the moment. Miss Pleasant was still eating, but her eyes were on him. Even Cecil's chewing had slowed, his eyes fixed on her father.

"We got the Brits to turn loose of the land. Since we couldn't negotiate the thing with the Colombians, it's just good luck that Panama revolted and got its independence."

"With American aid," Mrs. Tanner put in, interrupting him gently.

"Well, of course," Alexia's father said impatiently. "But whatever it took, the Colombians were persuaded to leave the Panamanians alone. If Secretary Hay can make some real progress with the sanitary conditions, we'll see that big ditch before long."

"It might not be as likely as all that," Mrs. Tanner said, her voice bantering, her smile cordial.

"More likely than women getting the vote, I would think," Alexia's father said. "Even though a canal would be a thousand times more useful."

For a second Alexia just stared at him, unable to believe he had said something so rude. He knew about Mrs. Tanner's work to get women the vote. He knew her opinions inside out. He was insulting her because he meant to do so. There was no other explanation.

Mrs. Tanner looked annoyed, but she didn't speak. Instead, she lowered her eyes to her plate.

"Tell us about your new position, Papa," Alexia said into the silence.

Her father glared at her, and she could feel her heartbeat in her temples. "There is little to tell as yet," he said slowly and distinctly, his expression warning her that she was not to pursue the subject. Alexia's heart constricted. Her fears were true, then. The new position had been a lie.

"It would seem that everyone is a little sensitive today," Miss Pleasant said in a voice that was meant to give everyone a graceful way out of the conversation.

Alexia's father stared straight at Mrs. Tanner. "I only wish you could play us a soothing melody after dinner." Alexia could not believe that he had said it, but he went on. "That would be the very thing to ease all of our cares."

"I once performed for all my friends, Mr. Finsdale," Mrs. Tanner said, her voice curt and coldly polite. "But no more. Now I can barely play the scales up and down. As you well know." She stared at him a moment more. "Your daughter has said that she might enjoy learning."

Alexia watched her father from the corner of her eye. She had told him how much it bothered Mrs. Tanner that she couldn't play anymore. A new thought came to her. Maybe he really did have a new position—and so he wasn't worried about provoking Mrs. Tanner. Alexia felt an uneasy mixture of discomfort and hope.

"Music lessons are a fine thing for a girl Alexia's age," Mrs. Tanner pressed. Her face was stern and set. Alexia knew her well enough to know she was fighting her own feelings of bitterness to suggest that Alexia should have lessons. It was so unfair that someone so skilled with her hands should be in so much pain and have so much difficulty using them.

"I agree with you entirely," Alexia heard her father say to Mrs. Tanner.

Mrs. Tanner did not answer him. She ate the rest of her meal in silence.

Alexia helped Cook clear the table. Her father waited until she had finished. Everyone else had left the dining room immediately after the meal. They had all looked uneasy, Alexia thought.

"I am going out for a while," Alexia's father said, once Cook had finished clearing and was back in the kitchen filling the basin with hot water from the copper-lined tank on one side of her woodstove.

Alexia nodded, wishing he would leave. She wanted to go talk to Mrs. Tanner. She had looked so upset by the end of dinner. She had limped back up the stairs with her head high and her shoulders square and stiff. Even the twins had been quiet as they left. And poor Cecil had looked miserable.

"Did you hear me, Alexia?" her father asked impatiently.

"I did," she said, turning to face him. "You said you were going out."

He nodded. "I have to go find out a few things about my new position."

Alexia looked into his eyes. He looked absolutely sincere. If he did have a new position, then everything was probably going to work out. If she could find a way to keep him from drinking—especially in the daytime.

"I'm sorry I drank the beer today," he said, as though he could guess her thoughts.

Startled, Alexia dropped her eyes. It was so hard to tell when he was lying and when he was sincere.

"I suppose I've just been worried about losing my place at the printers." He ran a hand back over his hair and sighed. Alexia reached out and took his hand. He met her eyes. "You look more and more like your mother, Alexia. I miss her so much."

Alexia nodded, her eyes stinging. "I have been so scared all day."

"I have too, Fairy Princess," her father said. "I went clear out into the western addition this morning, to talk to a man who is going to solve all of our problems."

Alexia let him pull her close in a hug. His coat smelled of tobacco smoke. His voice was soft and reasonable and full of love for her. "I apologize for losing the print shop position. I know I said I would keep it. But the shop just hasn't been busy enough for Mr. Cole to keep me on."

He held her out at arm's length to look into her eyes again. "But now that I have this opportunity, everything is going to be just fine."

Alexia smiled tentatively. "What is it, Papa? What new business?"

He grinned. "It's in the medical field. Medicinal compounds. If it all goes right, and it will, in a week or so, we ought to be able to leave."

Alexia caught her breath. "Leave?"

"I have a wonderful opportunity for us, Alexia.

With a little capital and a little luck, they say a man can make a fortune right now in concrete."

Alexia stared at him. "Concrete? Like the sidewalks? I thought you said medicine—"

Her father nodded. "To get our stake together. But concrete is the future. There is talk that it is going to be more useful than anyone ever thought it could be. There are men working on figuring out how to use it to pave whole roads." He paused. "Or telephones."

"Concrete telephones?" Alexia said, before she could stop herself. She felt breathless, as though someone had knocked her down, hard.

Her father laughed. "No, just plain telephones, made out of wood and brass. They are the wave of the future, too. A man could make a mint. I would need investors . . ."

Alexia had heard this kind of talk all her life, and it had always scared her. But today, there was another feeling rising inside her—anger. She searched for a way to tell her father that she didn't want to leave, that they had to stay here. Her life was just beginning to feel steady—like it might go on for a while. And now he wanted to go off again, moving to God knew where.

"I'll be back in a few hours," he said, releasing her and stroking her cheek. "Don't you say a word to our dear Mrs. Tanner yet, all right? I want to tell her myself, once everything is set."

Before she could say anything more, he had turned and was leaving, walking straight out the front parlor door. Alexia could only stare, watching him go. After a moment, she could hear him whistling as he made his way down the street.

CHAPTER TEN

Alexia sat on the edge of her bed. She felt sick. She had taken her diary out, but she couldn't seem to write anything—what was there to write? That her father was about to leap into some scheme and they were about to move again? She touched the red silk cover. She didn't even want to open her diary. If she did, she would see the entry she had written that morning.

How could she have been so silly? Her life wasn't going to change. It would be the same forever. Her father would take them from one town to the next forever and—

"Alexia?"

Mrs. Tanner's voice broke into her thoughts and Alexia was grateful. She stood up quickly and went to open the door. "Yes?"

Cecil was standing behind Mrs. Tanner. His cap was in his hands and he was smiling.

Mrs. Tanner had an anxious expression on her face. "I forgot to ask your father if he minded your going to the Galleno market for me. But Cecil says he will drive you up there on his way back to work. So you would only have to be alone coming home. It's a perfectly safe walk midday. What do you think?"

Alexia took a deep breath. What she really wanted to do was to tell Mrs. Tanner that her father wanted to leave. But she knew he would be angry if she did.

Mrs. Tanner was watching her closely. "I would send Amy, but one of her little ones is sick and she must get home to check on her, then return to start supper."

"I am happy to go for you," Alexia said, sorry that her hesitation had made Mrs. Tanner feel awkward about asking the favor.

Mrs. Tanner sighed gratefully and Alexia could see the relief in her eyes. "Thank you. I really don't think I could manage it. Ask Mr. Galleno to add this to my account. Tell him I will come and pay soon."

"I don't mind at all, Mrs. Tanner. Neither would Papa. I walk that way alone all the time during school." Alexia was trying hard to keep her voice normal, but her feelings were spinning in tight circles. She did not want to leave. She had to think of a way to make her father want to stay, too.

Cecil was turning his hat around in a circle. "I'm ready now if you are."

Alexia nodded. "I'm ready."

Cecil ducked his head in a little bow, gesturing toward the stairs. Mrs. Tanner turned slowly, walking so haltingly that Alexia stared. Her limp was much worse.

"I told her she should lie down with it up on a pillow," Cecil said. "That's what the doctor told my father to do when he broke his anklebone."

"I will go and try your remedy this very minute, Cecil," Mrs. Tanner said over her shoulder. "Take good care of our Miss Alexia. She is precious to me."

Mrs. Tanner did not pause or speak again. She made her way across the reception room, going so slowly that Alexia glanced back at Cecil rather than watch her painful progress. He was turning his hat again. Alexia heard Mrs. Tanner open her apartment door. A second later it closed behind her.

"You should get your cloak," Cecil said. Then

he blushed, but only a little, and he didn't duck his head.

Alexia turned back into her room, realizing abruptly that her diary was out on the bed. She scooped it up and slipped it into the trunk in a motion so smooth and so swift that she hoped Cecil had not noticed. She pulled her cloak from the hook by the door and grabbed her hat. She was still adjusting both as they went down the stairs.

"Here's her list," Cecil said suddenly as they went out the front door. "I almost forgot." He fished in his shirt pocket and brought out a square of paper. "That would have been awful."

"You would have remembered before we got there," Alexia assured him as she took it from him. Mrs. Tanner had said once that Cecil had grown up on a farm and was shy because he had not been around many people besides his own family.

Cecil was wonderful with animals, that much was sure, Alexia thought as they crossed the porch. Perseus leaped up to receive Cecil's passing touch, and the pair of geldings hitched to Cecil's delivery wagon turned to look the instant they heard his voice. One of them nickered softly.

"Brownie and Tolly have been working hard today," Cecil said to Alexia as they crossed the little yard. "Six loads of flour before dinner." He held her elbow as she climbed onto the driver's bench. She ran her hand over it, wondering if she should have brought a cushion—but the wood was smooth. It wouldn't damage her dress.

Cecil backed the team around, watching to see that the wagon wheels didn't roll into the deep ditch on the far side of the street. The horses were calm and paid attention to every flick of the reins. Cecil talked to them almost constantly, his voice serious, as if he expected them to answer.

It was strange to be riding in a wagon—especially one as big and heavy as this one. Alexia glanced back through the slats and saw a big squarish shape, covered in canvas. Ropes crisscrossed the bulky object.

"What is it?" she asked as they rounded the corner and started up Howard Street. She pointed back over her shoulder when Cecil glanced at her.

"A piano. A woman up on Nob Hill is donating it to the Dolores Mission."

"Do the Chinese girls like piano music?" Alexia wondered aloud, thinking about what Mrs. Tanner had said about rice flour.

Cecil looked surprised. "Who wouldn't?"

Alexia smiled at him. He was absolutely right. Of course the girls at the mission would enjoy the piano. They would all probably learn to play. She scooted forward on the seat, putting the thought out of her mind. She would never take piano lessons. It wasn't something her father would want to pay for and they would probably be leaving Mrs. Tanner's lodging house before long anyway.

"I'm sorry your father was so . . ." Cecil began. He was blushing furiously, Alexia saw. "I mean, I could tell you were . . ." He shook his head and mumbled an apology.

Alexia pulled in a deep breath. "It's all right," she managed, but then she looked down Howard Street, staring blindly at the buildings ahead of them. The steps in front of the lodging houses were dotted with groups of men standing and talking. Some of them smoked cigars. Most of them would be going back to work shortly, Alexia knew.

Cecil pulled a watch out of his waistcoat and looked at it. He put it back, frowning. "I'm running a little late." He clucked at his team and they responded, breaking into a slow trot. Alexia kept scanning the groups of men. Maybe Papa was among them. Alexia glanced at Cecil. It was possible—maybe even likely—that her father's *opportunity* in medicinal compounds was a fib. Maybe Cecil's employer needed more wagon drivers.

Alexia started to ask, then didn't. What was the point? Wagon driving would be too plain for her father. He would hate it, just like he had hated his job at the printers. It would only be a matter of time before he got news of some new scheme—or got into trouble of some kind—or both.

Without warning, a dog shot out of some bushes, barking frantically. "Steady on, Brownie," Cecil called out. The horses held their pace, even though Alexia could see the white rims around their eyes as they tried to look back at the dog that ran so close that it was almost under the wagon. No one called the dog off. It ran like a crazed thing, snarling and snapping at the rear wheel.

Abruptly, the dog seemed to notice the front wheel. It sprinted forward with a fresh spate of sharp barks. The gelding on that side was unnerved at last. It sprang forward and Cecil fought to pull it back, the reins singing with strain as he hauled back on them. Its harness mate bolted a second later and Cecil was pulled upright as the reins were jerked forward.

The wagon rumbled heavily behind as the terrified horses swerved, galloping up Howard Street. The piano slid from one side of the wagon bed to the other. A carriage driver saw them coming and pulled out of their path, glaring at them as they thundered past. His passengers were an elderly woman and a small child, Alexia saw. The woman didn't even look up. The child looked startled.

Alexia hung on to the iron rail that ran along the back edge of the driver's bench, Mrs. Tanner's list crumpled in her hand. She stared at the ground as it blurred beneath her feet. The dog was still yipping madly, running alongside the horses now, nipping at their tails. A man with a handcart loaded with vegetables wheeled it onto the sidewalk to get out of their way. He spilled some of the produce and yelled after them, shaking his fist in the air.

Alexia glanced back at Cecil. His freckled face had gone dead white. The tendons in his neck stood out like cords and his forearms were bulging with effort, but the team was too scared and too strong for him. He shouted at them to ignore the dog, to settle back, but the grinding roar of the wagon drowned out his voice. Some ragged kids playing kick the can looked up. A few shouted at the dog. Most just stood silently, watching.

Fighting the sway of the wagon, Alexia looked down at the dog. Its tongue was out, dripping with saliva, its teeth bared in a snarl. Without thinking, she leaned down a little ways, shouting at it. It ignored her. Shoving Mrs. Tanner's crumpled list into her bodice, she pulled off her hat. The hair pins pricked her scalp as they came loose.

"Get away," she screamed at the dog. "Go on!"

She threw the silk roses from her hat at its face as hard as she could. With a startled yelp, the dog bounded aside, front legs stiff, skidding to a stop. Alexia saw it stand alone in the street, staring at the roses at its feet. Then it looked wistfully at the wagon. Finally, it turned to trot back toward the lodging houses.

"Hold up now, Brownie. Hold up, Tolly. It's gone now. You hold on up!" Cecil's forehead was shiny with sweat. Alexia faced front. They were getting close to Third Street. Cecil shouted again, and Alexia heard him grunt with effort as he tightened the reins.

Finally, the team began to slow. When they dropped from a canter back into an uneasy trot, Alexia realized she had been holding her breath and exhaled.

Cecil turned to grin at her. "You saved that piano. Maybe our lives with it." He was breathing hard, and she could see welts where the hard edge of the reins had been dragged across his palms.

Alexia was breathing as hard as the horses were. "I was scared," she admitted.

Cecil was looking at her with pure admiration. "You didn't scream or get silly like a lot of girls would do. You ran the dog off."

Now it was Alexia's turn to blush. "You had your

hands full. I thought I had better do something."

Cecil nodded, clenching his right hand into a fist over and over. Alexia could see a little blood along the edge of the welt.

"Good, Brownie," Cecil called out. "And steady, old Tolly. That dog scared the oats out of both of you, didn't it?"

Alexia felt giddy as they turned right onto Third Street. She almost laughed aloud.

"I'll take you to Galleno's, then I'll go get your roses."

"That will make you late," Alexia said, shaking her head. "I can pick them up walking back."

"Someone else might get them first," Cecil argued.

Alexia shrugged. Pushing her hair back out of her eyes, she shook her head once more. "I found them in the throwaways at Mrs. Tanner's shop almost a year ago. If they are gone, I will just retrim the hat someday."

Cecil looked relieved and nodded. He reined the horses in across from the three Italian markets.

"I can manage from here," Alexia said after Cecil had helped her down. She smoothed her skirts and smiled.

"I feel like I ought to stay and drive you back to the lodging house," Cecil said.

Alexia shook her head. "Then you'd run behind time at work, for certain. I'm fine. I'll be back home in less than an hour."

Cecil hesitated a second more, then got back up on the bench. "Don't dawdle anywhere, though. You'll worry Mrs. Tanner if you do."

"I won't," Alexia promised. She waited until Cecil had turned the team and started back up Third Street before she pulled the list out of her bodice and started across the street.

The bell fastened to the door jingled merrily as Alexia went into the middle grocery. She inhaled the scented air as she let the spring close the door behind her. She was still feeling odd and light, like she could fly. Cecil had said she was brave. Was she?

The grocer was stacking figs in a basket. His white shirt and rolled sleeves were clean and crisp. The figs were big and purple, and Alexia felt her mouth flood with saliva. She rarely ate fruit, but she loved it when she could. She watched him working for a moment before he looked up.

She nodded politely. "Hello, Mr. Galleno."

"Good day," he answered cheerfully. Just then, a little boy with long dark curls came running in from the back of the store. He was wearing knickers—with little silver buckles beneath his knees. He whispered something, then ran back. The grocer laughed aloud, shaking his head. "One moment more," he said to Alexia. "Then I will be pleased to help you."

Alexia smiled and nodded. The Galleno brother in charge of this store was the elder one, and he always reminded Alexia of a friendly lion. He was big and broad with a deep voice. He had a little gray in the temples of his dark hair but it still curled like a boy's, shiny and falling over his brows.

"Yes?" Mr. Galleno said, placing the last fig on top of the pyramid. He turned to look at her. She held out Mrs. Tanner's list.

"This is for the seamstress lady, yes? Mrs. Tanner?"

Alexia nodded. "She said you would bill her?"

"She has come here for years. I trust her for this."

He touched his forehead in a small salute. "Give me a few minutes to make sure I have everything she wants. I can send the wagon around in an hour. Right now the boy is out delivering."

"I'll wait," Alexia said.

"Salted or unsalted butter?" the grocer asked, looking at the list.

Alexia shrugged. "I'm not sure. What does she usually get?"

"Salted," Mr. Galleno said. "Half a tub."

"I think that's what she meant, then," Alexia told him.

Mr. Galleno went back to reading the list, looking up from it now and then to see what was on the shelf or to check the level in a bin or a barrel. He used a big tin scoop to dip the snow-white Occident Bread Flour up out of its bin into a cloth bag. He packed the brown sugar into a square wooden box.

Alexia stood watching, wondering if he had forgotten that she was waiting. Finally, he lifted the list one last time and read through the items once more. "I have everything, I am sure now," he said. "You can go on home and tell Mrs. Tanner that the wagon boy will come soon with everything she wanted."

"I will," Alexia said, starting for the door.

"She told me about you," Mr. Galleno said from behind her. "You are the one she teaches to sew?"

Alexia turned back to face him. He was looking at her, smiling, leaning back against one of the enormous cracker barrels that lined the wall. "We were talking one day. She is very fond of you."

Alexia swallowed hard, surprised at the sudden painful constriction in her throat. She tried to make a polite answer, then had to cough a little. She managed to bid Mr. Galleno a good day, smiled, and went out the door.

On the sidewalk the sun had paled and Alexia shivered. The evening fog was coming in. She started down the sidewalk, wishing her father hadn't allowed them to stay here a whole year. It was only going to make it harder to leave when the time came. She would miss the twins and Mr. Chair with his leather cases of shoes. She would miss Cecil, too, and his kind heart. Alexia blinked back tears. She would miss Mrs. Tanner most of all.

CHAPTER ELEVEN

Alexia hurried along the sidewalk, glancing behind herself now and then to make sure none of the rough-voiced kids from the transient hotels was sneaking up on her. They had never hurt her, but they were terrible about teasing, following her halfway home before they would let up.

She watched for her roses, trying to remember where they had been when she had thrown them. Alexia scanned the lodging houses. Had they been opposite the Lormor? Or farther down by the Ohio House or the Nevada House? All the transient hotels had men standing around outside during dinner break. Now, almost no one was around.

She saw a tiny flash of red half a block ahead of her on the sidewalk. She was sure the roses had landed in the street, but she walked a little faster anyway. As she got closer, she could see them, laid neatly on the edge of the curb.

She picked up the bedraggled silk roses and looked around, wondering who had moved them. Whoever it was had been kind. The roses were dusty from the cobblestones, but they were intact—and the dust would brush off or dry clean out with a good rubbing of fine white flour.

Alexia took off her hat and tucked the roses back underneath the ribbon, then put it back on. She turned a circle once more, but no one caught her eye—no one seemed to notice her at all. She sighed. It would have been nice to be able to thank someone before she went home.

Alexia found herself walking slower and slower, until she was just creeping along, letting other people on the sidewalk bustle past. Carriages and wagons rolled by, and Alexia could hear a few words of people's conversations as they passed. Usually, she liked to listen, to imagine what people's lives were like. Today, nothing seemed fun or interesting.

Alexia kicked at a stone. She missed and

scuffed the sidewalk hard enough to make her toes hurt for a few seconds. She felt foolish and couldn't stop tears from brimming her eyes. It was going to be awful at home. Mrs. Tanner wouldn't be working anymore today, not with her ankle aching and swollen. It would be at least an hour before Cook needed help.

Alexia turned up Langton Street—and her heart froze. Her father and two other men were standing on the next corner, talking. Alexia stopped, staring. One of them was the man from Market Street—the red-faced man who had bumped Mrs. Tanner. Alexia felt a crawling sensation on the back of her neck. The other man had a long drooping mustache. It was the man she had seen with her father in the morning, she was sure of it.

Impulsively, Alexia dodged behind a eucalyptus tree and pressed close to the papery bark. She peeked around the trunk. Her father was gesturing, talking in a voice too low for her to hear. He jabbed one finger into the air, looking fiercely into the eyes of the red-faced man. Then he punched a closed fist upward, and his voice rose just enough for Alexia to hear two words.

"Your fault . . ."

Then he hushed himself, looking around.

His features were contorted with anger. He stepped a few paces away. The other two men shifted and Alexia noticed a black leather bag beside the mustached man. It looked like a suitcase—or a doctor's bag. Alexia felt the prickle crawl across her neck again. A doctor? Why would her father be standing here arguing with a doctor?

A little breeze blew through the eucalyptus and the leaves rattled like gray-green paper. Alexia squeezed her eyes closed, then opened them again, straining to hear.

"Now we are going to have to . . ." her father was saying—then another breeze rustled the stiff leaves.

Alexia sank down from her tiptoes, feeling an ache in her cramped feet—and in her heart. What was going on? The voices suddenly got louder and she looked again. They were walking toward her.

Alexia instinctively moved around the tree trunk, positioning herself so she was hidden. The footsteps became clearer, closer. She could hear her father first.

"You're going to have a lot more trouble with this than Fish would have. It's as simple as that."

"But, Mr. Finsdale, I . . ."

The breeze rose, blotting out her father's next few words. Then his voice rose about the rustling of leaves.

". . . know nothing at all about medicine, O'Leary."

Alexia crouched down behind the tree where the trunk was thickest, her heart thudding. Her father was insulting the doctor. Why?

After a moment of silence, Alexia risked peeking out once more. The three men had gone past her and had stopped again, this time at the corner of Howard Street. Her father was standing with his shoulders squared, his feet set in a fighting stance.

The red-faced man was talking now, his rough, grating voice impossible to mistake—but impossible to understand. Alexia held her breath, willing the breeze to still so that she could hear. But it didn't.

Alexia saw her father walk away from the other two men twice. Both times, they called him back. It was obvious that whatever the argument was about, he was winning, wearing them down and persuading them. Alexia recognized the quick flash of his smile when they gave in. She exhaled slowly. What was going on? Were these men somehow involved in her father's medical compound opportunity? Surely the doctor was, at least. Or maybe they were both doctors. But why had her father argued with them?

Alexia poised herself, ready to step out the moment they went on around the corner onto Howard Street. Her knees trembling a little, she waited, moving just enough to catch a glimpse of her father walking toward her again. They weren't leaving. They were coming back.

Alexia ducked, listening to the footsteps pass one more time. Then the sounds of leather soles on the gritty cobblestones faded completely. Alexia counted to fifty. Then she leaned out a little ways, moving an inch at a time. The sidewalk was empty.

Alexia eased out from behind the trunk and stepped onto the sidewalk quickly. Walking as briskly as she could manage, Alexia headed home. Halfway there she noticed a thin strand of bark stuck to her cloak. She brushed it off, nervously checking her skirt for more as she turned to cross the little yard.

The shop was still closed. Mrs. Tanner was almost never even mildly ill and it was hard for Alexia to picture her lying down, in pain. The image was disturbing and Alexia pushed it aside as she went in the front door and started up the stairs. Halfway up, she heard her father talking. Then Mrs. Tanner.

Alexia slowed her step, trying to hear what

they were saying. As she got high enough to see, she slowed even more. Her father was standing with Mrs. Tanner and the mustached doctor. The black leather bag was sitting on the floor between them. The red-faced man was nowhere to be seen.

"Alexia!" Mrs. Tanner called, spotting her. "I was beginning to worry."

"I told her you were fine," her father said, smiling broadly. "She doesn't know how you can dawdle, does she?"

Alexia swallowed in a dry throat. "I guess not," she said, climbing the last stair and stepping into the reception room. Mrs. Tanner was leaning on the back of one of the Morris chairs. Her brow was creased with discomfort.

"Is your ankle worse?" Alexia asked her.

Mrs. Tanner smiled. "It will improve in a day or so."

"I am trying to get her to allow Dr. Norris to examine it. He says that proper treatment of this kind of sprain can be critical."

Alexia looked at the doctor. Norris? Her father had called him something else before, hadn't he? An Irish name? He had accused him of knowing nothing about medicine, too. So why was he recommending him to Mrs. Tanner?

"Help me talk some sense into this landlady

of ours, Alexia."

Alexia realized she had stopped and was still holding on to the bannister post. She took a step toward her father and Mrs. Tanner, then another. The doctor was staring at her as she approached them. She glanced past them. Where had the red-faced man gone? Alexia's stomach tightened. Her father was smiling.

"Alexia? Did you hear me? Help me talk sense into Mrs. Tanner."

"I think it would be wise if you would allow me to look at your ankle," the doctor said smoothly. "We can do it right here. I needn't disturb your clothing more than an inch or two—"

"And I would be happy to leave you in privacy with your physician," Alexia's father broke in, smiling. "But will you please let him? It was a stroke of luck that I ran into him at the Corona House after all these years—on the very day that we needed his services so badly."

Mrs. Tanner glanced at Alexia, then back. "Well, all right. It can't hurt anything, and you say there will be no charge?"

"Of course not," Doctor Norris said quickly. "I am happy to help a woman my old friend so admires."

"You are both far too kind," Mrs. Tanner

said, leaning on the chair as she made her way around to the front of it. She sat down, dropping into the seat like a boy would, clearly unable to support her weight on her injured ankle.

"Alexia will stay with me," Mrs. Tanner said.

Alexia watched her father nod. "Of course. I will wait in the parlor downstairs. Thank you, Fairy Princess," he added, brushing his hand across Alexia's cheek as he went past.

Alexia, startled by his touch, stepped back. He smiled and started down the stairs. Halfway down, he turned back and called out to her. "Come and talk to me when they are finished, will you, please?"

Alexia nodded numbly, not sure what she should do or say. Her father acted like he was trying to do Mrs. Tanner a favor—maybe he was hoping that she would consider the free doctor's visit a value against their rent? Had he changed his mind about leaving? Her throat ached with hope even though she knew it was unlikely.

"I will just need to extend your limb—sit back and close your eyes and relax, please," the doctor was saying.

Alexia glanced once more after her father. Then she went to stand by Mrs. Tanner's chair. "That's perfect," the doctor was murmuring. Mrs.

Tanner had followed his instructions. Her eyes were closed and her face as relaxed and peaceful as it had been since she had fallen. He was touching Mrs. Tanner's ankle. She made a little sound of pain when he angled her foot to the right. He applied a little pressure in the opposite direction and Mrs. Tanner made the sound again.

"Be more careful," Alexia said sharply.

For an instant there was a look of anger on his face, but then he smiled. "I am being very careful, miss. I am simply trying to find out— where the problem is."

Alexia stared at him as he opened his bag. He took out a stethoscope and hung it around his neck. Then he removed a roll of white cotton bandage cloth. His hands, Alexia noticed, were trembling slightly. He flexed Mrs. Tanner's foot again and she winced. Alexia bit her lip, uneasy. Was he a good doctor or some saloon fake her father had talked into giving a false examination? He might, if he thought it would buy time on the back rent. She tried to recall everything she had overheard, tried to make sense out of what was going on.

"It's not broken," the doctor said reassuringly.

Mrs. Tanner opened her eyes. "I am glad to hear that. It was hurting so much that I was beginning to wonder."

"Will you hold this for a moment?" He held out the roll of bandages. When Mrs. Tanner extended her hand to get it, he made an exclamation of sympathy. "Oh, I am so sorry to see that you suffer from arthritis."

Alexia glanced toward the stairs involuntarily. Her father had made such a point of discussing Mrs. Tanner's arthritis at dinner. What was going on?

"I have had some pain with it all of my adult life," Mrs. Tanner was telling the doctor. "Lately it is worse."

He clucked low in his throat. Then he looked up, meeting Mrs. Tanner's gaze with a look of extreme concern. "The danger is the deforming and crippling of the fingers and hands."

Mrs. Tanner nodded. "I am afraid that I will soon have hands like lobster claws, bent and useless."

Alexia stared at her.

"I am sorry for you to hear my bitterness," Mrs. Tanner said quickly. "I apologize, Alexia. One so young should not have to hear the complaints of the old."

"You aren't old," Alexia said quickly.

"That hurts a little, Doctor," Mrs. Tanner whispered. He was holding Mrs. Tanner's hand, staring down at her fingers. He asked her to close her hands into fists—then to open them. He directed her to extend only her index fingers, then to spread all her fingers as widely as she could. He watched her hands the whole time, studying her movements.

"Does that hurt?" he repeated over and over.

"Yes," Mrs. Tanner answered every time, "a little."

Alexia could tell that each stretch of her fingers hurt more than she was admitting.

"I have some days that are better than others," Mrs. Tanner said when he finally released her hands. "It has been bad all this week. I think it's the damp. It seems to get worse when the fog comes in every morning."

He nodded. "Do you do any activity that involves the fine use of your fingers and thumbs?"

Mrs. Tanner hesitated. "She's a modiste," Alexia answered, feeling strange, as though she was standing on a ferry with the deck rolling beneath her feet. "She sews by hand a great deal, also by machine."

"Why do you ask, Doctor?" Mrs. Tanner's voice was muted.

He looked up. "There is a treatment used in Japan. An ancient compound made with herbs they grow there. The conflict in the region has made it expensive to obtain. But it seems to hold great promise for people such as yourself if used early enough in the condition."

Mrs. Tanner sat straighter. "What is the herb?"

Alexia bit at her lip. This was wrong. This had something to do with her father, and it was wrong.

The doctor smiled and fiddled with something in his bag before he looked up. "There are several. The main ingredient is Shenawa Toka." He glanced toward the stairs, then at Alexia. "It is quite safe," he said. "A simple herb that one drinks in an infusion of hot water. You can also soak rags in the hot tea and wrap the affected part before the cloth cools. I have seen impressive results."

Alexia watched Mrs. Tanner's eyes begin to sparkle. "People are cured of arthritis?"

He nodded. "Sometimes. My colleague said the remarkable thing is that the joints go back to the free, elastic movement of youth when the tea is used long enough."

Alexia could only listen, wishing with all her heart that this was true—that her father wasn't trying to cheat Mrs. Tanner. But in her heart she knew it was all too much of a coincidence to be true. But how could he do this? He knew what Mrs. Tanner meant to her.

"This cure was seen by someone you trust?"

There was a girlish edge in Mrs. Tanner's voice, and Alexia could see a wild spark of hope in her eyes. She tipped her head back to smile at Alexia, wrinkling her nose like a child inhaling the smell of a flower. "That is very hard to believe, sir," she said, looking back at him.

"Nevertheless," the doctor said, "it seems to be so. I expect that within a few years they will have the cure in this country, easily purchasable at any drugstore."

Mrs. Tanner sat back. "A few years?"

The doctor nodded. "Until then there are only a few places to obtain it. My friend is one source. I have been getting small amounts of the herbs for two of my patients."

"And what is the cost of the herb?" Mrs. Tanner asked. She reached up to take Alexia's hand.

"It can be very costly."

"How costly?" Mrs. Tanner asked again.

"A hundred dollars for a month's supply." He said it very distinctly, glancing up at Alexia, then toward the stairs, then up at the ceiling. Alexia heard Mrs. Tanner pull in an astonished breath at the same time she did. A hundred dollars. That was a small fortune. Alexia scrutinized his face. How much of that hundred dollars was to be her father's? Oh, how could he?

"It is almost cruel to mention such a cure," Mrs. Tanner said, and Alexia could hear the anger and bitterness in her voice.

The doctor was unwinding the bandage. He began to wrap her foot, his movements awkward and clumsy. His hands were still trembling. He finally finished and tucked the end underneath the last spiral of cloth. He fiddled with his stethoscope. Alexia realized suddenly that he hadn't used it at all. The bandage came untucked and he reached down to redo it. Once he was finished, he stood up abruptly. "Go tell your father we are finished."

Alexia was startled. "Mrs. Tanner—" she began, knowing that she had to warn her, had to tell her that this was almost certainly a scheme, a cheat, even if it meant having to leave and never seeing her again. "Mrs. Tanner, I have to—"

"—get your father, dear," Mrs. Tanner interrupted her, smiling. "Then we'll talk. I have to think about everything the good doctor has told me."

Alexia turned numbly and started toward the stairs. With every step the tightness in her stomach was hardening into anger. If this hundred-dollar herb was her father's *opportunity*, she was going to find out about it. And she was going to tell Mrs. Tanner.

CHAPTER TWELVE

"Where did you meet Dr. Norris?" Alexia asked her father the instant she stepped off the bottom stair. He was sitting in the overstuffed parlor chair. He looked up from the newspaper he was reading and folded it across his lap. "In St. Louis. Why, Fairy Princess?"

"I just wondered." Alexia looked down, struggling to keep her voice steady. "I don't remember him, Papa."

"He was around when you were still a baby."

"You have never mentioned him. Or a Mr. O'Leary." She watched her father's smile stiffen. "Where's Mr. Fish?" Alexia asked, watching his face.

His eyes went wide. "How do you know about Fish?"

Alexia felt her eyes flood with tears, but she forced them back. "What are you doing, Papa? Why did Mr. Fish knock Mrs. Tanner down?"

"Alexia—" Her father reached out to touch her cheek but she backed away.

"No. I want to know what you are doing. Is Dr. Norris really a doctor?"

Alexia's father didn't answer. He was studying her face. "No," he said finally. "He isn't. Fish used to be, almost, in the army. He was a medical supply officer."

Alexia stared at him.

"Fish was going to try to strike up a conversation with Mrs. Tanner when he bumped into her. He was just going to notice her hands, tell her about the herb, and she would never have known I was involved at all. The ankle was an accident. We never meant to hurt her." He shook his head. "Fish was so upset he couldn't think fast enough to simply act the part of a doctor then and there."

"But, Papa—" Alexia began.

"I owe Mrs. Tanner a great deal of money," he interrupted. "I thought this way we could—" He stopped, and Alexia could only shake her head as she began to understand.

"See, Alexia, this way we take her money and give most of it right back to her," he said in a low voice. "That's all. She'll buy O'Leary's herbs and he'll keep a small part of the money. Then we give the rest back to Mrs. Tanner, our rent is caught up—and tomorrow or the next day, we can leave. We'll have enough left to get to—"

"—it's stealing," Alexia interrupted him.

Her father took her hand. "No, it isn't. Of course it isn't. I told you, we give the money back. Most of it."

"It's stealing, Papa. And it's cruel. She believes him." Alexia pointed upward. "She is sitting up there, so full of hope and—"

"What's wrong with hope?" Alexia's father said, a little too loudly. Then he continued in a harsh whisper. "Alexia, there is nothing wrong with this. No one gets hurt."

"Mrs. Tanner does, Papa," Alexia said dully. And me, she wanted to say. Why couldn't he see that for himself? Alexia could feel her own pulse drilling at her temples. Her father just stood there looking at her as though this was a normal discussion all girls had with their fathers. He looked offended at her silence.

"Mrs. Tanner doesn't know anything is odd, does she?"

"No, Papa," Alexia said sadly. "Is that your only concern? You're going to keep a lot of the money, aren't you? This was your opportunity, wasn't it? Your surprise for me. A cheat."

He frowned at her, putting on one of his actor's faces—this one was reasonable, but stern. "If you can't be sensible, Alexia, then you will just have to be obedient. Stay down here. I am going to go up. O'Leary—Dr. Norris—might need me."

Without another word he turned and strode away, not looking back. Alexia followed, stopping at the bottom of the stairs. She could hear her father's voice, then O'Leary's, but she couldn't understand what they were saying. Alexia put her foot on the bottom stair, straining to hear.

"Alexia? Are you there?" It was Mrs. Tanner, calling her from above.

Alexia took in a quick breath. "Coming," she called back, bounding up the stairs. Her father turned to glare at her, but she brushed past him to go stand beside Mrs. Tanner.

"I am going to try this Japanese arthritis cure," Mrs. Tanner said, smiling up at Alexia.

"Shenawa Toka," O'Leary said.

Mrs. Tanner repeated the two words, shaping her mouth around them as though they were prayers. She shot another smile at Alexia, then lifted her head and addressed Alexia's father. "Dr. Norris says that if I give you the money tomorrow morning, you'll carry it to him at the Corona where he is staying?"

"That would be fine," Alexia's father said. Alexia stared at him as O'Leary said his good-byes and left, his fake doctor's bag swinging from his hand as he went down the stairs.

"Let me help you to your room," Alexia's father said. "You look a little fatigued." He offered Mrs. Tanner his arm and she let him ease her up out of the Morris chair, then lead her across the thick red carpet. It was obvious that every step on her injured ankle caused her a lot of pain. Alexia stood watching helplessly. What if it really was broken? Now she wouldn't go to a real doctor to find out.

Alexia knew she should say something now, before her father managed to spirit Mrs. Tanner away—but she was still hoping she could find a way to make her father stop the scheme without having to tell Mrs. Tanner. Then they might be able to stay.

At her apartment door, Mrs. Tanner stopped and turned. "Alexia? Will you help me a minute? I think I will just put on a wrapper and lie down."

Alexia saw her father's face darken. She nodded, looking at Mrs. Tanner. "Of course." She started across the reception room just as Cecil came clumping up the stairs. Perseus was walking behind him, meowing for Cecil's attention. Cecil picked him up as he smiled at Alexia's father and Mrs. Tanner.

"I had to come back this way with a load and I wanted to make sure—" Then he saw Alexia and grinned. "I told them all at work what you did. They said you have a quick wit and—" He glanced up at Mrs. Tanner and Alexia's father. "Didn't she tell you?" Cecil blushed, but he managed to tell the story.

"Alexia!" Mrs. Tanner said admiringly when he finished. "We'll see you driving an automobile with a scarf tying your hat down yet. You see how brave you are?"

"In two years there won't be any more automobiles," Alexia's father scoffed, smiling.

"Alexia told me you think they have no future. I disagree."

"Mark my word," Alexia's father said. "They will disappear entirely."

Mrs. Tanner nodded vaguely. "Forgive me. I need to lie down. Thank you for coming to make sure Alexia was safe, Cecil." Cecil grinned once more, still holding Perseus. Then he turned and went down the stairs.

Alexia heard Perseus's meow of complain when Cecil set him down at the foot of the stairs. She could feel her father glaring at her, but she refused to look at him even once as she guided Mrs. Tanner inside and closed the door behind them. She knew if she let him smile at her, his handsome face boyish and pleading, that she might lose her resolve.

Once they were inside Mrs. Tanner's room, Mrs. Tanner limped to her bed and sat down on the edge. "My father," Alexia began, then stopped. She looked out the window and stared at the fog gray sky. "My father is trying to cheat you." The words came out in a rasp. "The doctor isn't a real doctor. He's some friend of Papa's and . . ."

Mrs. Tanner made a little sound of pain and Alexia looked at her. She lifted one hand to wave away Alexia's concern. "I thought it too good to be true. I just . . . hoped."

"I hate him for doing this to you," Alexia whispered. Then she shook her head. She didn't hate him. She couldn't.

"No, you don't," Mrs. Tanner said, patting the bed beside her. Alexia went to sit down and Mrs. Tanner took her hand. "So Dr. Norris—"

"His name is O'Leary. Mr. Fish was a medical supply officer in the army. Or at least that's what my father said." She explained everything, including Mr. Fish's mistake in bumping her.

"Well, I should have known," Mrs. Tanner

sighed, lifting her hands to look at them.

"My father says we are leaving in a couple days. Please don't call the police."

Mrs. Tanner looked startled. "Leaving?"

Alexia nodded miserably. "Papa said it before—when we were downstairs. He wanted to pay you the rent with your own money, then leave with the rest. Will you tell the police?"

Mrs. Tanner was silent for so long Alexia began to fidget. When she spoke her voice was even, measured. "No. Not if he leaves." She leaned forward. "But listen, Alexia. You could stay. He could come to visit and write you letters. I will teach you my trade—like an apprenticeship." She looked at Alexia.

Alexia was stunned. "I don't want to leave. I have been so upset and scared and I . . ." Finally, the tears that had been aching behind her eyes spilled over. She cried hard, and Mrs. Tanner managed to get up and limp toward her, her arms extended. Alexia leaned against her, unable to stop crying for a long time. When she finally did, Mrs. Tanner kept hugging her as she sniffled and wiped at her eyes.

"I am afraid to ask him," Alexia finally whispered. "He won't let me stay."

"This is your decision," Mrs. Tanner answered.

"He loves you and I think he will understand. You must live your own life, Alexia."

Alexia took a step back as Mrs. Tanner released her. Her own life. Did she have one? She hated the way Papa lived, fibbing to everyone they met. For an instant she imagined it—staying with Mrs. Tanner, never having to leave, learning to sew, having her own money—her own life. She drew in a ragged breath. "I want to stay. More than anything."

Mrs. Tanner nodded. "I'm glad. I want you to."

Alexia took another deep breath. This one was a little steadier. "I better go talk to him. Before my courage fails."

Mrs. Tanner patted her hand. "It won't."

Alexia went out, crossing the reception room to her own door. It was slightly ajar and she hesitated an instant, then swung it open. Her father was standing at the window, looking out.

"Papa?"

He turned quickly. His face was unreadable, his eyes searching hers. "Did you tell her?"

Alexia nodded.

He smacked her mother's trunk with an open palm. "Why? Now you've ruined everything. Alexia, how could you do this to—"

"How could you cheat Mrs. Tanner? How

could you just lie to her like that?" Alexia blurted out the questions before she could stop herself. "You know I love her. How *could* you?"

His face darkened. "Alexia, I'm your father. Don't talk to me like—"

"I'm staying here," Alexia said in a shrill voice, to make him stop.

He stared at her. "What?"

"If you leave, she won't call the police." Her eyes stung but she willed herself not to cry. "She says I can stay on and learn how to sew—like an apprentice. And I want to, Papa." Alexia drew in a breath and met his eyes. "I'm not going with you."

He looked at her for a long time without speaking. Then he nodded slowly. "I always said that woman was a bad influence on you." He paused. "She's not going to involve the police?" His voice was even, measured, as though he were discussing business. But his eyes were soft and sad like when he talked about her mother. He looked out the window, then, finally, faced her again. "I'm glad you found your roses."

She blinked, confused, then understood. "You put them on the sidewalk?"

He nodded. "Cecil is right. You're quite a girl."

Alexia stood silently, unable to speak. After a long silence, her father crossed the room in three quick strides and hugged her tightly, then turned and walked out the door, closing it very quietly behind himself.

Alexia ran to the window. She saw him come out the front door, squaring his hat on his head. O'Leary was across the street, waiting behind the dusty lilac hedge. Together they walked toward Howard Street, talking. Alexia saw her father turn and look back twice. Then they were gone.

Papa promises to write me, to never go anywhere without letting me know in a letter. He didn't cry, but I did. I feel as though I have been crying for days. I walked him down to the corner and we stood under the eucalyptus tree and talked a few minutes more before he went.

I have made three decisions:

I am going to work very hard at my trade.

I am going to treat Mrs. Tanner as a stepmother. She is that to me, and more.

Cecil and the twins and Mr. Chair are my family. I care very much for all of them and am going to be as good to them as I can—but I am going to write my mother's sisters soon. They might want to know where I am and how I am doing. I would love to receive news of them.

Mrs. Tanner's ankle is a little better. If it is not much improved by tomorrow, she says she will go to a real doctor and find out if it is broken. I hope it improves. She has enough pain—it seems unfair that she should have to bear more.

It is sunny this morning. Bright and blue

and no fog at all. This is the saddest day of my life. But maybe it will be the beginning of my happiness.

I watched Papa walk up Howard Street. After a half block or so, he started whistling. I could hear it faintly. He turned once to wave at me. I stood there until I couldn't see him anymore. It is so strange to think that he will not be back today, or tomorrow, or for a long time. I will miss him terribly, but I know I am right to stay here. Mrs. Tanner said I have my own life. This morning, I am beginning to believe that is true.